Airdrie

D0894795

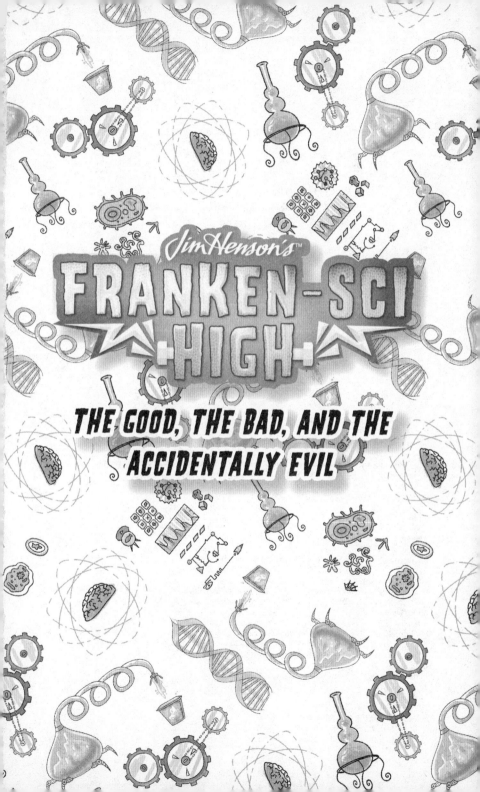

Jim Henson's™
FRANKEN-SCI HIGH

THE GOOD, THE BAD, AND THE ACCIDENTALLY EVIL

What a wonderful road we've traveled to get to here—
this amazing series wouldn't be in our world without you.
This is for you, Halle. —M. Y.

This book is a work of fiction. Any references to historical events, real people, or real places are used fictitiously. Other names, characters, places, and events are products of the author's imagination, and any resemblance to actual events or places or persons, living or dead, is entirely coincidental.

SIMON SPOTLIGHT
An imprint of Simon & Schuster Children's Publishing Division
1230 Avenue of the Americas, New York, New York 10020
This Simon Spotlight hardcover edition December 2020
© 2020 The Jim Henson Company. JIM HENSON'S mark & logo, FRANKEN-SCI HIGH mark & logo, characters, and elements are trademarks of The Jim Henson Company. All Rights Reserved.
All rights reserved, including the right of reproduction in whole or in part in any form.
SIMON SPOTLIGHT and colophon are registered trademarks of Simon & Schuster, Inc.
For information about special discounts for bulk purchases, please contact Simon & Schuster Special Sales at 1-866-506-1949 or business@simonandschuster.com.
Designed by Ciara Gay
Manufactured in the United States of America 1120 FFG
10 9 8 7 6 5 4 3 2 1
ISBN 978-1-4814-9146-4 (hc)
ISBN 978-1-4814-9145-7 (pbk)
ISBN 978-1-4814-9147-1 (eBook)

Jim Henson's FRANKEN-SCI HIGH

THE GOOD, THE BAD, AND THE ACCIDENTALLY EVIL

CREATED BY **MARK YOUNG**
TEXT WRITTEN BY **TRACEY WEST**
ILLUSTRATED BY **MARIANO EPELBAUM**

Simon Spotlight
New York London Toronto Sydney New Delhi

The Search Is Over

Newton Warp stared up at the tall, brick dormitory surrounded by palm trees and colorful tropical flowers. It was a typical day on the island—sunny, hot, and humid—but Newton didn't mind. He'd always liked hot weather, but now he suspected it was due to his lizard DNA.

Newton had been staring at the building for fifteen minutes, afraid to go in. Because when he went in, he knew he'd have to tell either a big truth or a big lie to his best friends, and either way, it was going to be bad.

A fly landed on his nose, and his tongue instinctively lashed out. He'd almost pulled the fly into his mouth, when he realized what he was doing, and he flicked it away.

They did this to me, he thought. *I'm a monster, created in a lab, to do a job. I'm not human, like them.*

He gazed around the courtyard, at the other students

1

at Franken-Sci High. Boris Bacon was bouncing across the ground in his antigravity boots. Rosalind Wu was circling the courtyard in a jet pack. And Tootie Van der Flootin was walking a fluffy yellow monster with three eyeballs, on a leash.

How nice it must be, to be a normal human. To know not just who you are but what you are. To only be worried about what's for lunch in the cafeteria and whether you'll pass your next teleportation test.

Newton had never known that feeling of being normal. The first feeling he could remember was being confused and a little scared, when he had appeared in the library of the school for mad scientists, with no memories of where he'd come from and with a strange bar code on his foot. Luckily, Shelly and Theremin were the ones who'd found him, and the animal-loving girl and her robot buddy had become his good friends.

He'd met more friends too, like his roommate, Higgy, who was made of green goo. And Odifin, a talking brain in a jar, and Odifin's assistant, Rotwang. And lots of other kids were nice to him, even Mimi Crowninshield, who was usually mean to other people. In most cases, having friends would be enough to make somebody feel like everyone else. But not Newton.

Newton's first friends, Shelly and Theremin, had

quickly realized there was something different about him. He had abilities that normal humans didn't have. He could blend into the background when he was afraid, and sprout gills that let him breathe underwater, and change his appearance to mimic other people—and those were just some of the special things he could do. Newton had uncovered memories of being born in a pod, with scientists gathered around him. Did that have something to do with his weird talents?

Shelly and Theremin, along with Higgy, had promised to help Newton figure out where he'd come from, who his family was, and why he was different.

After some digging, smart thinking, and sneaking around, they'd learned a few things. Time-traveling Professor Flubitus had admitted that Newton and Shelly played an important role in the school's future. And Flubitus had also delivered the news that Odifin and Newton shared some significant DNA, basically making them half brothers.

Then, today, Newton and his friends had made the biggest discovery of all. They'd found a science fiction book called *The Invincible Man* about a scientist who spliced human and animal DNA to create an indestructible, human-looking creature in a pod. The character in the book sounded just like Newton! But that wasn't the

4

most mind-blowing part. The author's name was Zoumba Summit, and Newton had figured out that when you scrambled the letters, they spelled "Mobius Mumtaz"— the name of the headmistress of Franken-Sci High.

Armed with that information, Newton had confronted Ms. Mumtaz, Professor Flubitus, and some of the other professors in the school. And he'd learned some truths. Yes, Mumtaz had written the book. And years in the future, the book had inspired her to create Newton in a lab. The professors had worked together to splice animal DNA and human DNA, and had made Newton in a pod so that he could save the school. Then they'd wiped his memory of being created, and dumped him in the past, in the library.

Not a real human. No real family, Newton thought now, still staring up at the dorm.

And after dropping that bombshell, Mumtaz had refused to say any more. She couldn't tell Newton *how* he would save the school, because that could change the outcome of the future.

"And, Newton, you mustn't share this knowledge with your friends. It could jeopardize everything we've worked for," Mumtaz had added.

Newton didn't care one lick about what those professors had worked for. He had been fully prepared to tell

his friends everything. But then Professor Phlegm, with his shiny bald head and sinister eye patch, had thrown out a threat: a memory wipe.

The more Newton thought about it, the more his part-reptilian blood went cold. The professors had wiped his memory before dumping him in the library, and he'd made a lot of memories since then—good ones as well as bad ones. Was Phlegm threatening to take away *all* his memories? Without them, he'd lose his friends. And what if the professors wiped his friends' memories too? Or kept the friends away from one another, so that they couldn't become friends again? The worries swirled through his mind.

Newton sighed. He knew what he had to do, and it wasn't going to feel good. He walked across the courtyard and into the dorm. He stepped into the glass transport tube and said, "Freshman floor."

Whoosh! The tube shot up four floors and then opened. He stepped out and made his way to the door marked YTH-125. He paused a moment before opening the door. Then he took a deep breath and entered.

"Newton!" Shelly leaped off a chair, making her curly hair bounce, and pounced on him in a hug. "Higgy said that Mumtaz called you to her office because of what happened in London, and then she kicked Higgy out as soon as you mentioned Zoumba Summit. What did she tell you?"

"I wanted to stay and listen through the door, but the drones carried me back here," Higgy said. He was sitting on the bottom bunk, with no clothes on his body, which was made of green protoplasm. Higgy had recently decided to stop hiding his gooey self in layers of clothes and bandages, which was why they had gotten in trouble in London.

"Like always, Mumtaz didn't tell me anything," Newton lied. "She said it was just a coincidence that her name is an anagram of 'Zoumba Summit.'"

Odifin wheeled up to him. "And you believe her?" he asked, his voice crackling from the speaker attached to the jar of liquid that held him.

Newton shrugged. "I don't know. But she made it pretty clear that there's no point in asking any more questions. All we really know is that the future of the school depends on me and Shelly. We're going to have to wait for the future to get answers."

"That's not fair!" yelled Theremin. The robot's eyes flashed red. "We need answers. You need answers! I say we go to her office and demand them."

"Yeah," agreed Rotwang. His messy black hair hung down over his eyes, as usual.

Newton held up his hands. "No!" he yelled, and his friends all looked at him, surprised. Newton hardly ever yelled. "We've wasted too much time searching for answers that we're never going to get. I just want to have a normal life."

"But don't you want to find your family?" Shelly asked.

"No," Newton said, and it was easy to sound convincing, now that he knew he didn't have one. "No, not anymore. I have you guys. That's enough."

Shelly hugged him again and the others joined in. "That's so sweet, Newton."

"I'll always be your bro, bro," Theremin said. "But are you sure you don't want to keep looking?"

"I'm sure," Newton said, and he looked at his friends, one by one. "Let's just put all this behind us, okay?"

"Okay," everyone answered, although Shelly was avoiding Newton's gaze.

"Isn't there some big event coming up?" Newton asked. "Let's just have fun doing whatever that is."

"As a matter of fact, Founders' Day is coming up," Odifin replied. "It's a big celebration honoring the founding of Franken-Sci High."

"See, that sounds like fun!" Newton said. "So let's all get ready for Founders' Day and try to forget all about

the future and that other stuff for now. Okay?"

Shelly frowned. "Okaaaaay," she said slowly. "I need to go check on my animals in the basement. See you all at dinner?"

"Certainly!" Higgy said. "In fact, I might head to the cafeteria right now for a snack. All this excitement has made me hungry."

"Since when have you needed excitement to make you hungry?" Theremin teased. "You're *always* hungry!"

Higgy patted his green belly, which jiggled. "I need a lot of energy to keep this protoplasm in top form."

"I'll go with you, Higgy," said Rotwang. More than six-feet-tall and as skinny as a test tube, Rotwang could eat more than anyone else *not* made of green goo.

"I suppose I'll join you," Odifin said. "I can people-watch while you eat."

Theremin turned to Newton. "What do you say, bro? Want to maybe play some laser hockey?"

Newton yawned. "Not right now. I'm kind of tired from London and everything. I'll catch up with you later."

"Sure, bro," Theremin said, and the room emptied out. He climbed up onto the top bunk and let out a long breath. He hated lying to his friends, but at least they would all be safe now. And he could wait a few decades to find out why the professors had created him, right?

Bing! The tablet in his sweatshirt pocket made a notification noise, and Newton took it out. A holographic envelope projected from the screen, and Newton touched his finger to the seal. The words popped out and hung in the air in front of him.

NEWTON,

YOU ARE INVITED TO A TOUR OF CROWNINSHIELD INDUSTRIES NEXT SATURDAY AT 10 A.M. A PORTAL PASS WILL BE PROVIDED FOR YOU.

MIMI CROWNINSHIELD

Newton stared at the invitation. Mimi had always puzzled him. He'd seen her be super mean to Shelly, but she'd been polite to Newton and seemed interested in him. He had no idea why she wanted to invite him to her family's company headquarters, but it would give him something to do besides worry about the future. He pressed the yes button on the hologram, and holographic confetti popped out. Then the hologram disappeared.

Mimi, what are you up to now? Newton wondered.

CHAPTER 2

Crowninshield Industries

"Mimi, what are you up to now?" Shelly asked Mimi the next day in the hallway, after Newton had told her about Mimi's invitation.

Mimi's blue eyes widened, making her look innocent. "Why on earth would I have something up my sleeve?" she asked. "My family's company is preparing some very special surprises for the Founders' Day celebration, and Newton is my friend, so I thought he'd like to see them. He didn't get to go on the tour with the freshman class like everyone else did last summer."

Shelly frowned. "Seriously? I'm supposed to believe that you have no ulterior motives for this nice gesture?"

Mimi sighed. "Shelly, I know you and I haven't always gotten along, but you have to admit that I've never done anything bad to Newton, right?"

"Well . . ." Shelly's voice trailed off.

"Anyway, Newton already said he wants to come,"

Mimi pointed out. "And when he comes back, I'm sure he'll tell you he had a great time."

"Hmpf!" was all Shelly could say in response, and she turned on her heel and walked away, her crocheted snake scarf flapping behind her.

Mimi grinned. "So trusting, Shelly," she whispered. "So trusting . . ."

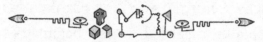

The week passed by quickly, and Newton was surprised at how normal things felt, compared to what had happened since he'd come to the school. Well, things were normal by Franken-Sci High standards.

Every day, he licked his locker security panel to identify the flavor so that he could open it. The week's flavors were hot licorice, liverwurst, chocolate-covered mushroom, garlic, and banana-blue-cheese.

Every day, he went to class. In Physics of Phys Ed, he swung on ropes over a pit of hybrid shark-crocodiles. In Quantum Emotional Chemistry for Nonemotional Chemistry Students, he worked on a Beautiful Sadness formula—the kind of sadness you feel when you watch a movie about a heroic dog or when you see a sunset and are sad that the day is over even though the sky looks beautiful. And in Retro Robotics class, he actually had fun making an old-school mini windup robot.

Every day, he ate in the cafeteria. He tried new dishes invented by the cafeteria cooks. Peanut butter balls with so much protein in them that they came to life and bounced up and down on their own. A kale salad that tasted like pepperoni pizza. Chicken wings that flew right into his mouth.

Yes, it was a normal week at Franken-Sci High, all right, and Newton settled in and began to enjoy himself. Sure, the knowledge that he was a genetically engineered being was always in the back of his mind, poking at his brain cells, but he pushed it aside.

Then Saturday came, and Newton reported to Ms. Mumtaz's office at 9:55, five minutes earlier than Mimi had asked him to. He knew Mimi didn't like lateness. The door was open, and Ms. Mumtaz was sitting at her desk. She stared at Newton through her cat-eye glasses.

"Hello, Newton," she said. "How's everything going?"

"Just fine," he said, staring right back at her. "Everything's perfectly normal. Like nothing weird ever happened."

She nodded, bobbing her head like a bird, which wasn't surprising. With her long, thin, neck and slim, pointy nose, she had always reminded Newton of a bird.

"Glad to hear it," she said. "I'm glad to see you've calmed down, Newton. Nothing to do now but look forward to the future."

"Sure," Newton replied, although inside he was thinking, *You mean the future that's going to be a disaster unless I somehow stop it with my freaky powers!*

"Good morning, Newton!"

Mimi entered the office, neatly dressed in a denim skirt, sneakers, and a white collared shirt with a blue vest over it. Her blond curls bounced on her shoulders.

"Uh, hi, Mimi," he replied.

Mimi held out a hand to Ms. Mumtaz. "We're ready for the portal pass, please," she said.

The headmistress handed a paper brochure of the school to Mimi. Mimi opened it all the way into a big square. Then she folded it into smaller and smaller squares. Finally she folded it diagonally so that the top left and bottom right corners touched.

The tightly folded brochure began to spin, and floated out of her hands. As it spun faster and faster, it created a rotating column of air. Newton's wavy hair whipped in front of his eyes. Then the whirling stopped, and a portal with a halo of glowing light appeared where the brochure had been.

"Ladies first," Mimi said, and she stepped through

the human-size hole and quickly disappeared.

"Have fun, Newton!" Ms. Mumtaz called out as he stepped through the portal behind Mimi.

Newton blinked. They had emerged into the bright sunlight. The portal closed and Mimi caught the brochure before it hit the ground. Then she tucked the brochure into her skirt pocket and gestured in front of her.

"Come on! We can take the funicular to the top of the mountain," she said, and she ran ahead.

Newton looked up and saw a gleaming, white building on top of a tall mountain in front of them. A sign with large, black letters announced: CROWNINSHIELD INDUSTRIES: THE FUTURE IS IN OUR HANDS.

Newton wasn't sure what a funicular was, but he guessed it might be the thing that looked like a white train car that Mimi was running toward. It was rectangular, with large windows on all sides. He followed her inside, where she announced "Main gate!" and the door slid shut behind them. Then the train car made its way on a track, winding toward the top of the mountain.

"I've always thought we should put a teleport pad down here. It would be so much faster," Mimi said. "But Mom and Dad insist that we keep the *mad*-scientist stuff we do top secret. To the rest of the world, Crowninshield Industries is just a top company in technological

innovation—like the low-emissions auto fuel we've been perfecting." She sighed. "Maybe one day we won't have to hide our real genius. But I guess the world isn't ready for us yet."

"No, I guess not," Newton agreed absentmindedly, watching the scenery. They were surrounded by mountain peaks on all sides, and the view got more spectacular the higher they went.

Finally the funicular stopped at a platform in front of the white building. The car's door slid open automatically, and Mimi and Newton hopped out.

They walked up to the building's large, glass doors, and Mimi slid an ID card into a receptor on the wall. There was a buzzing sound as the doors opened.

The chill of artificially cooled air hit Newton as they stepped into a hallway with a white floor, white walls, and a white ceiling. The hall opened into a lobby with a circular desk, where a woman sat, surrounded by computer screens.

"Hello, Satoko!" Mimi greeted her.

The woman smiled. "Mimi! Good to see you. We're expecting you."

"This is my friend Newton Warp," Mimi said, and Newton nodded. "I'm going to introduce him to Mom and Dad."

Satoko shook her head. "Sorry, Mimi. They're in

meetings all morning. Didn't they tell you?"

Mimi's face fell for a second, but she quickly put a smile back on. "Nope. Guess they forgot. Anyway, I'm going to give Newton a sneak peek of what we're doing for the Founders' Day carnival."

"Have fun!" Satoko said. She pushed a button, and a swinging, waist-high gate opened up next to her.

Mimi led Newton down another hall.

"Sorry you won't get to meet my parents," Mimi said. "They're really, really busy."

"That's okay," Newton said. "They do a lot for the school."

Mimi grinned. "Yeah, wait till you see what I'm about to show you."

She stopped in front of a clear tube—the same kind of transportation tube they used at Franken-Sci High. Mimi noticed him noticing.

"Look familiar? Yeah, these were invented here at Crowninshield," she said, and she and Newton stepped inside.

Whoosh! The tube sucked them up to the top floor of the building. They emerged in front of a large metal box, open on two ends, with a conveyor belt running through it. Mimi walked up to a control pad and started pressing buttons.

"This is a top secret research floor," she said. "Everyone gets a body scan when they enter, to make sure you're not bringing in pathogens that could damage the equipment."

"Does it hurt?" Newton asked.

Mimi laughed. "Of course not! Watch. I'll go first."

Mimi stepped onto the conveyor belt, and laser lights scanned her body from her head to her feet as she moved through the machine. She stepped out on the other side.

"Your turn!" she told Newton.

Newton moved through the scanner, and Mimi was right—it didn't hurt a bit. They walked to more glass doors, which Mimi opened with another card. This led them to a catwalk looking down over an enormous, wide room.

Down below, workers wearing white lab coats scurried about, working on enormous contraptions, the likes of which Newton had never seen before. There were flashing lights, bright colors, and mechanical animals.

"What's all this?" he asked, his eyes wide with wonder.

Mimi grinned, pleased with his reaction. "These are the rides for the Founders' Day carnival," she said. "Each year, Crowninshield Industries provides different rides, and each year we make the rides better and better."

She walked down the catwalk, and Newton followed. She stopped at a giant transport tube shaped into a series of twisted loops, like a giant, mutant pretzel.

"We call this the Dimension Destroyer," Mimi said. "It's like a roller coaster, but the ride takes you through six different alternate dimensions."

Newton's mouth dropped. "Whoa."

Mimi continued walking and pointed to a circular ride with colorful wooden horses attached to poles.

"Looks like a regular merry-go-round, right?" Mimi asked. "But watch. The horses are sophisticated robots programmed with precise horse movements and the ability to navigate around objects."

One of the workers climbed onto an orange-and-pink painted horse, music began to play, and the circle spun. The horse suddenly whinnied, jumped off the carousel, and began to trot around the research floor.

"That looks fun," Newton remarked.

"Wait until you see the next one," Mimi said, and she broke into a run. She stopped and pointed to the floor, at what looked like a large, plain white box with an entrance and an exit.

"That looks pretty . . . ordinary," Newton remarked.

"We need to jazz up the outside," Mimi said. "But look what it does. We call it the Customizer."

A worker stepped through the entrance. The box shook, and yellow lights flashed from inside. When the worker emerged from the other side, she wasn't wearing her white coveralls. Her hair was pink, her skin was purple, and she wore a green dress with a yellow lightning bolt on it.

"You know how when you play a video game, you can collect different looks for your avatar and change your appearance with just a tap of a button?" Mimi asked. "Well, this does it in real life, instantly!"

Newton stared at the purple-skinned woman. "Is it permanent?"

"No. That's the best part," Mimi said. "You just have to walk through again to go back to your usual appearance."

Newton shook his head. "Mimi, this is awesome! You're always talking about how amazing your parents' company is, and you're right! This is so cool."

Mimi smiled proudly. "Thanks, Newton. I'm glad you like it. Come on. Let's see some more."

They walked the catwalk all the way around the research floor, and Mimi pointed out some of the other attractions in the works.

"A lot of it's pretty simple, like the antigravity bouncy house," she said. "But that one's always a big favorite."

"This is all really great," Newton said. "So, what other kinds of inventions does Crowninshield make? Can I see some of them?"

Mimi shook her head. "Sorry. That's all top secret," she said. "But I *can* show you the cereal bar in the cafeteria. There are fifteen different flavors, and none of them are slug or mustard."

Newton laughed. "Thank goodness!"

They ate in the cafeteria, and then headed back down the mountain in the funicular. Taking in the mountains and the blue sky, Newton felt a pang. He didn't want to leave.

"Mimi, I really want to thank you for taking me on a tour," he said as they stepped out of the portal and back into the school hallway. "It was really nice of you."

"You're welcome," Mimi said. "Be sure to tell Shelly that. She thinks I'm mean."

"Sure," Newton said. "See ya, Mimi!"

He waved and walked off. When he was out of sight, Mimi turned on her tablet and pulled a small flash drive from her skirt pocket. She plugged the drive into the tablet and grinned as text appeared.

Downloading body scan of Newton Warp . . .

CHAPTER 3

Two Perfect Plans

Shelly couldn't believe that Newton was giving up on the search for his identity. She'd watched him all week, licking his locker pad and swinging over shark-crocodiles and eating in the cafeteria like he was just another student at Franken-Sci High.

Something must have happened that day he talked to Mumtaz, she'd thought. *He'd been so focused on finding his family and figuring out why he has those special abilities. Why did he suddenly stop?*

She'd asked Theremin about it, but he didn't think it was a big deal.

"I think Newton was just tired of feeling different," Theremin had said. "I know what that's like."

And when she'd talked to Higgy, he'd had another idea. "Newton knows that Odifin is his half brother. And Newton has us. He doesn't need to look for his family anymore."

But Shelly still wasn't convinced. She didn't want to stop trying to figure out the mystery of Newton Warp. The professors at the school knew something, she was sure of it. But how could she keep asking them questions without looking suspicious? And without making Newton upset? She puzzled over this for a few days, and then at the end of the week, it came to her. She announced her plan at dinner Saturday night, after Newton had returned from Crowninshield Industries.

"I've got the best idea," she said, while Newton, Theremin, and Higgy listened. "We're going to start the *Franken-Sci Herald*!"

"You mean a newspaper?" Higgy asked.

Shelly nodded. "A holographic newspaper, digitally sent to the tablets of everyone in the school once a week. We can write about school events, and exciting inventions students are coming up with, and we can interview professors. . . ."

"That sounds interesting," Newton said.

"It sounds like a lot of work," Theremin mumbled.

"Come on. It'll be fun," Shelly said. "I already asked Mumtaz if we could do it, and she loves the idea. She's letting us use lab 27X as a newspaper office, and she wants the first edition to come out soon. So you guys *have* to help me. Please?"

"Hmmm," Higgy said. "I've always thought I'd make an excellent food critic. Can I write a food column?"

"Sure!" Shelly said. "Whatever you want."

"Well, I guess if we have to help, I always thought I'd be a great detective," Theremin said. "I've got built-in investigative equipment—heat sensors, matter detectors, scanners. I'll dig around for an explosive story to write about."

"Sounds great!" Shelly said. "I think I'm going to do a profile of a different professor in each issue. I've already set up an interview with Professor Leviathan."

Newton frowned. "What about me? I've never even read a newspaper, so I'm not sure what goes in it."

"We'll find a cool job for you," Shelly promised. "The first meeting is tomorrow at three. I'm going to send an announcement to everybody's tablet, so maybe we'll get some more volunteers, and we'll figure out other things to do."

"Excellent!" Higgy said, and he slid out of his chair. "I shall need some second helpings so I can start working on my first food review."

Shelly stood up. "And I'm going to interview Professor Leviathan," she said. "See you tomorrow!"

Shelly took the transport tube downstairs and made her way to Leviathan's lab. She stepped inside the cozy but messy room decorated with illustrated posters of plant and animal species. Beakers and petri dishes balanced precariously on piles of paper on a large desk, and sitting at that desk was a large woman with a wild mass of pink, curly hair.

She beamed when she saw Shelly. "You're right on time!" she said, in her booming voice. "Marvelous idea, this newspaper of yours. But you always have good ideas, Shelly."

"Thanks, Professor Leviathan," Shelly said, sliding into a chair in front of the desk. She turned on her tablet. "Do you mind if I record this interview?"

"Not at all," Leviathan said, smoothing down the wrinkles in her leopard-print lab coat. "I'm very flattered that you've chosen me for your first interview."

Shelly had actually chosen her because she thought Leviathan's friendly nature might make it easier to get information out of her. But she didn't say that.

"Well, you know how much I love your class," Shelly said. "Now, let's see. First question: How long have you been teaching at the school?"

"It's been about twenty years, I suppose," Leviathan answered.

Shelly leaned closer. "And in twenty years, have you noticed any secrets here at the school?"

Leviathan chuckled. "My, you're starting with the hardball questions, Shelly," she said. "But I suppose you're onto me."

"I am?" Shelly asked, surprised.

"Yes," the professor replied. She reached down and pulled open the bottom drawer of her desk. "If you've heard the rumors, it's true."

Shelly listened eagerly. Was she about to get the truth about Newton?

Leviathan pulled something out of the drawer and held it up—it was an ice cream pop, wrapped in paper.

"Yes, the bottom drawer of my desk is an ice cream freezer," she said, and she held out the pop. "Would you like one?"

"No thanks," Shelly said, holding back a sigh. "So, tell me more about the monster-making program here at the school. Have you ever experimented with combining animal and human DNA to create a monster?"

"Heavens, no!" Leviathan cried. "Only the maddest mad scientist would conduct an experiment like that. Most of what we do is based on combining the genes of existing monsters. Now, generally, real monsters are difficult to find, but you've had luck with that, haven't you, with your little friend, Peewee?"

As soon as the professor said the name, a small blue

monster appeared out of thin air on the desk between them.

"Peewee!" Shelly cried, and she picked up the blue monster. "How did you get out of your cage?"

Shelly had rescued the monster in the wild in the summer, and the creature had followed her to school without her knowing it. Professor Flubitus had mistakenly transformed the cute little monster into an enormous, terrifying beast. Thankfully, Peewee was back to normal, but he had the ability to teleport, which had gotten him into a whole new kind of trouble. Shelly had been putting him in a cage with a teleportation shield to keep him under control.

"Your teleportation shield might be on the fritz," Professor Leviathan guessed. "You should have your friend Theremin take a look at it, or see if Professor Yuptuka can fix it. I know Ms. Mumtaz won't be happy if Peewee starts teleporting everywhere again."

"I know," Shelly said, and she tucked Peewee under her arm. He wriggled his nose and made a happy, chirping sound.

"Now, what were you asking?" Leviathan wondered.

Shelly stood up. "I think I've got enough for now. I should go put Peewee in his cage."

"You do that," Professor Leviathan said, and then

she unwrapped the ice cream pop and ate it in one bite.

Shelly left the lab and hurried to the school basement, where she kept her animal rescue lab. She'd always been more interested in helping creatures than making them.

"*Shelly! Shelly!*" squawked a parrot with a robotic wing, which had replaced the one he'd broken.

"Hi, Wingold," Shelly said. "Do you have any idea how Peewee got out of his cage?"

"*Shelly! Shelly!*" the bird repeated.

Shelly put Peewee back in his cage and shut the door. She pressed the security button, and the light flashed green. She shrugged.

"Must have been a glitch," she said.

She spent an hour with the animals, changing their water and food and cleaning cages, while she thought about her interview with Leviathan. The professor had genuinely seemed shocked at the idea of creating something like Newton.

Maybe not all the professors are in on it, Shelly thought. *I'll just have to keep interviewing them until I get answers!*

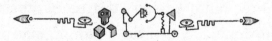

The next afternoon Shelly, Theremin, Higgy, and Newton met up in lab 27X.

"I'm sure we'll get some more volunteers," Shelly remarked right at three o'clock.

But only one more person walked through the door—Mimi Crowninshield.

"Mimi!" Shelly cried. "You want to be on the newspaper staff?"

"Why not?" Mimi asked. "After all, nobody knows more about the ins and outs of the school than I do."

Shelly couldn't argue with that.

"Great," Mimi said, taking Shelly's silence as acceptance, and then she sat on a stool next to Newton.

"So, what do you think you want to do for the paper?" Shelly asked Mimi.

"Well, a gossip column would be obvious, but I'm honestly not sure," Mimi admitted.

"Me neither," Newton confessed. "I'm not even sure if there's anything I can do to help with this."

Mimi's blue eyes widened. "Wait, I've got an idea!" she said, and she reached into her backpack and pulled out a device that looked like a metal doughnut. "This is the latest camera from Crowninshield Industries. It takes three-hundred-sixty-degree photos all on its own—you don't have to do anything except hold it! You could be the photographer."

Newton took the camera from her. "I guess I could

do it. This looks pretty cool. Do you think maybe you could show me how to use it?"

"Of course!" she replied. "We can walk around the school after the meeting, and I'll show you how. It'll be fun."

"Sounds good," Newton said. "I guess I'm the photographer, then!"

Mimi smiled, and not just because she had done a nice thing. She smiled because, like Shelly, she also had a plan. At first she hadn't been able to believe what she'd overheard about Newton the day she'd spied on him— that he'd been created in a lab and given enhanced abilities.

But the body scan had confirmed what she had heard. Newton wasn't entirely human. Some extra organs had shown up, and his DNA didn't match any human or animal in the computer's database. Mimi wanted to study Newton up close to see if she could witness his enhanced abilities, and joining the newspaper staff had seemed like the perfect way to do that.

"All right, then," Shelly said. "Theremin, I need you to help me work on a holographic publishing program."

"Sure," Theremin agreed. "After I work on my big scoop. I'm doing a piece on black holes in lockers, and how many students have gone missing."

"Great!" Shelly said. "Next we—"

"Good afternoon, newspaper staff!"

A huge holographic head of Headmistress Mumtaz appeared in the center of the room.

"Oh, hello, Ms. Mumtaz!" Shelly said.

"How is the meeting going?" Mumtaz asked.

"Pretty good," Shelly responded. "I think we'll be able to get out our very first issue on Wednesday."

"Excellent!" Ms. Mumtaz said. "And once you've worked out the bugs with your first issue, I'd like you to get started on a special edition that will be released on Founders' Day. I think our founders will be very impressed with this new addition to the school. I must confess that I'm quite anxious to please them, as last year they seemed disappointed in our lack of innovation—"

"Wait," Newton interrupted. "The founders of the school are the ones who started it, right? Wasn't that hundreds of years ago? Aren't they—"

"Dead? No," Mumtaz replied. "Their brains were among the first to be preserved in jars, like the brains in our Brain Bank. In order for the oldest brains to be preserved, they must remain in a dormant state, a sort of hibernation, for long periods of time. We wake up the founders only once a year. Which is why it is *very*

important that the event is a success this year. Do you understand?"

"Yes!" all the students answered.

"Very good," Mumtaz said. "I will leave you to your work. Carry on!"

Her holographic head disappeared.

"Wow," Shelly said. "A special edition for Founders' Day! I guess we'd better get this first issue out, and then we can start planning out the special issue."

Mimi stood up. "Newton and I will go take some photos now. Right, Newton?"

"Sure, Mimi," Newton said.

"Great," Shelly said. "Why don't you start with some photos of Professor Leviathan for the profile I'm writing?"

"Sounds good," Mimi said, and then she and Newton left the lab.

My plan is working perfectly! Mimi thought.

Shelly watched Mimi and Newton leave the lab. The special Founders' Day edition would give Shelly an excuse to ask the professors all kinds of questions.

My plan is working perfectly! Shelly thought, not realizing that Mimi had plans of her own.

CHAPTER 4

Smile and Say "Suspicious!"

"So how does this camera work?" Newton asked, turning the device around in his hands.

"It's foolproof," Mimi promised as they walked to Leviathan's lab. "Hold it in the palm of your hand. Then say 'click' when you want to take a photo."

The doughnut-shaped camera activated when Mimi said "click." It floated up from Newton's palm and began to spin in a circle.

"It automatically takes a three-hundred-and-sixty-degree photo of your surroundings," Mimi said. "And you can easily edit the photos if you don't want everything in the shot."

"Cool," Newton said as the camera landed back in his hand. "I think I'll be able to do this."

Mimi nodded. "It's so easy that a baby could do it!" she said. "No offense, Newton. That's just how it is."

I don't even know what it's like to be a baby, Newton thought, and then he scolded himself. *Stop thinking*

about stuff like that, or you'll never have a regular life!

When he emerged from his thoughts, Mimi was talking.

". . . after we photograph Professor Leviathan, we should go to some key areas around the school and get some photos for the special issue," she was saying. "That is, if you don't mind me tagging along."

"What? No, sure, that's fine," Newton said. "It's more fun than doing it alone."

They had reached Leviathan's office.

"Newton! Mimi! How can I help you?" Leviathan asked.

"Newton would like to take your photo for the school newspaper," Mimi answered.

"Yes, of course!" Leviathan said. She sat up straight in her chair, patted her pink curls, and smoothed out her leopard-print lab coat. "How's this?"

"Perfect!" Mimi said.

Newton held out the camera. "Click!" he said.

The camera lifted up and began to spin around. After one rotation it settled back onto Newton's hand.

"Now press the button on the top to project the photo," Mimi instructed.

Newton obeyed. An image projected above the camera, showing the professor, the lab, and Mimi—everything surrounding Newton.

"You can download it onto your tablet later, and then edit it just to have Professor Leviathan," Mimi said. "Or you could use the whole photo."

"That's very impressive," Professor Leviathan said. "Another product from Crowninshield Industries, Mimi?"

Mimi beamed. "You guessed it."

"Such a wonderful company," Leviathan said. "Although, I never understood why you don't have a monster division. Imagine what you could do with your resources!"

"My parents prefer to focus on nonbiological innovation," Mimi answered. "They're real tech heads."

"Ah, but imagine what you could do by melding monsterology with technology," Leviathan said. "I've got years of research behind me. With my knowledge and your resources, who knows what we could do?"

Mimi's eyes gleamed. "I like the sound of that, Professor. I'll talk to my parents about it."

"Excellent!" Professor Leviathan said. She stood up, and towered over both of them. "Do you need any more photos?"

Newton had been playing with the camera while they'd talked, talking more photos from different areas of the room.

"No, I think we're good," Newton said. "Thanks a lot!"

Mimi and Newton left Professor Leviathan's office. "Where to now?" Newton asked.

"Let's head to the gym," Mimi suggested. "I think some shots of the pool would be fun for the Founders' Day issue."

"Sounds good," Newton said. He rested the camera in his palm. Along the way, he stopped every few feet, taking photos of whatever looked interesting. An explosion of confetti and glitter in Professor Snollygoster's lab. Odifin zipping down the hallway with a green-and-yellow school scarf sailing behind him, tied to the pole underneath the table holding his jar. The cafeteria ladies trying to catch stalks of animated broccoli as they dashed around the kitchen.

"This is fun!" Newton remarked. "I think I'm getting the hang of it."

"You're a natural," Mimi said. "Let's get some shots of the pool, and then we can go back to the newspaper lab and I'll show you how to edit."

"Thanks," Newton said.

When they reached the gym, they made their way to the pool room, which had a blue tile floor and a big rectangle of water in the middle.

"Nobody's here," Newton said. "Maybe we should come back when kids are swimming."

"Why don't you get on the diving board to get a shot of the rippling water?" Mimi suggested. "That would be pretty."

Newton nodded. "Sure," he said, and he climbed the short ladder to the diving board and held up the camera.

"Get closer to the water," Mimi said, and Newton moved forward. "No. Closer."

Newton teetered on the edge of the board, which was just a foot above the water. Mimi climbed the ladder and stepped behind him. She had seen the fish DNA in his body scan report, and was curious to see how it worked. A little playful nudge might jolt that DNA into action. At least that was what she hoped.

"Hey, Newton!"

Higgy entered the room, and Mimi jumped back.

"Just came for a little dip," Higgy said. "Do you want to join me?"

"No, thanks, but I'd love to take your picture," Newton said.

"Sure!" Higgy cried, and he whipped off the towel from around his shoulders and jumped in. His green body floated on top of the water's surface.

"Look! I can do the backstroke!" Higgy cried as he splashed around the pool.

"Click!" Newton said, and the camera lifted off his

palm and spun around.

Mimi sighed. "Great shots, Newton. Let's get back to the lab."

Newton nodded. "Bye, Higgy!"

Mimi was quiet as they headed to the newspaper lab. Only Shelly was there, typing away on a terminal. She looked up when they came in.

"Hi!" Newton said. "I think I got some good photos."

Mimi took the camera from Newton and slid aside a panel. A short cord came out.

"You can link it to any computer or tablet, and you don't need a special app," she said. "The photos automatically download and create their own folder."

Newton linked the camera to his school tablet. A page popped up showing thumbnails of every photo he'd taken. He clicked on the first one he took after Mimi showed him how to use the camera. The photo showed Professor Leviathan at her desk.

"You just tap on the area you want to focus on, and a frame will pop up so you can crop," Mimi explained, showing him. "See? Perfect shot of Professor Leviathan."

Shelly looked up again. "I created a shared file for us on the school system. It's under 'Herald.' Can you upload the photo?"

Newton did just that, and felt a sense of

accomplishment.

Maybe photography is my thing, he thought, and that made him feel good. It was a talent that had nothing to do with his animal DNA. It was something *regular* kids did.

"It's time for dinner," Mimi said. "And I'm meeting some friends at the Airy Café. I think you've got this, Newton."

"I think I do," Newton agreed. "Thanks for the camera, Mimi."

Mimi grinned. "You're welcome. See you around."

Mimi left, and Newton turned back to the photos he'd downloaded.

"That was really nice of Mimi to give me the camera," Newton said to Shelly.

Shelly frowned. "I'm sure she has some ulterior motive. There's usually a catch when Mimi's being nice."

Newton shrugged. "Maybe. She seems like she's just being nice, though."

"Hmpf!" Shelly said, and then she cried out, "Peewee!"

Newton had seen the small blue monster just appear out of nowhere on the lab table Shelly was sitting at.

"How'd he get out of his cage?" Newton asked.

Shelly shook her head. "It happened before, and I thought it was a glitch. But I guess I need Theremin to take a look at the teleportation shield. There's a lot to do to get this issue out, though." She sighed and stood up. "I'm

going to go put him back in his cage. I'll be right back."

The monster squeaked as she picked him up and walked out the door, leaving Newton alone.

Newton started to examine the photos he'd taken. There was the sign in front of the school. There was Odifin zipping down the hallway. He swiped his finger on the screen, taking in the whole three-sixty view.

He paused on a head with a shock of green hair, peeking out from behind an open locker.

"Professor Flubitus?" Newton asked.

He tapped on a photo that he'd taken of the cafeteria ladies. There, behind where Newton would have been standing, was Professor Flubitus again.

Peeking into Snollygoster's classroom—Flubitus.

Behind Newton as he photographed a row of lockers—Flubitus.

Outside the door of the pool—Flubitus.

It's just like before, when he was following me around and I didn't know who he was! Newton realized. *But why is he doing it?*

There was only one way to find out. Newton quickly got up and went to look for the professor.

CHAPTER 5

Read All about It!

Newton found the professor in his classroom, where the man was seated at his desk, with his green hair standing on end. Newton didn't bother to be polite.

"Why are you following me again?" he asked.

"Newton, I fear you are mistaken," Professor Flubitus replied.

"Don't lie," Newton said. He thrust his tablet in front of the professor. "I have photographic proof."

Flubitus frowned. "All right, you've caught me. But honestly, Newton, I can't tell you—"

"You always say that!" Newton cried. "I already know that I was created in a lab to save the school in the future. So why are you secretly following me around?"

Flubitus nervously drummed his fingers on the desk. "As I've told you, Newton, I cannot tell you what is going to happen in the future," he said. "At least, I don't *think* I can tell you. There have been new developments

in the future, and I'm trying to find out exactly what is happening in this time line that would cause—"

Newton interrupted him. "What do you mean '*this* time line'?" he asked. "Are there other time lines? And what does that even mean?"

"Oh dear. You see, I've said too much," Flubitus said. "Traveling back and forth to and from the future will scramble your thoughts a bit, Newton. I don't recommend it."

"So let me guess," Newton said. "You're not going to tell me what happens in the future, or why you were following me?"

"Not right now," Flubitus said. "But . . . things may change, Newton. I ask you this, young man. Please give me some time for my brain to clear. I am sure I will figure things out."

"Fine," Newton said. "But I'll only agree if you stop following me."

The professor nodded. "I will. I'm sure . . . I'm sure there's nothing to worry about. I just need to clear my head."

"Okay, then," Newton said, but he felt uneasy as he left the professor's classroom. Normally he'd go looking for Theremin and Shelly to talk it over, but he couldn't do that now. From now on he had to keep everything secret—or risk losing them if the professors wiped their memories along with his.

The next day Newton and his friends met in the newspaper lab after school.

"I'm calling my food column Hungry Higgy's Food Review," Higgy announced, typing into a computer terminal. "For my first review I rank all the cafeteria's pudding flavors from best to worst."

"What's the best?" Newton asked.

"Butterscotch," Higgy replied. "And the worst is anchovy."

Newton shrugged. "I like that flavor," he said.

"Of course you do," Higgy said. "You'll eat anything weird."

"Maybe I would," Newton admitted. "But I've never eaten ten gallons of pudding in one sitting!"

Higgy nodded. "Fair," he said. "Okay, we're both weird!"

Newton looked over at Mimi. "How's your gossip column coming?"

"Great!" Mimi said. "I'm calling it Eye Spy on Franken-Sci High," she answered.

Theremin's eyes flashed green. "That's got a ring to it," he said. "So what's the hot gossip?"

Mimi cleared her throat. "Okay, here's an example. 'Which freshman has been *bacon* his roommate crazy with his sound barrier experiments? I don't see what the problem is. They might be loud and annoying, but they'll never *bore us*!'"

"I don't get it," Theremin said. "Which freshman is it? Why don't you just tell us his name?"

Mimi grinned. "That's how you write a gossip column. You don't say the name outright, but you give a clue."

Newton rolled it over in his mind. *Bacon his roommate crazy . . . never bore us . . .*

"It's Boris Bacon!" he cried.

"Right!" Mimi cried back.

"Very clever, Mimi," Higgy said.

"Sure, it's clever," Theremin said. "But wait until you see the story I'm working on."

Theremin walked up to Shelly, who was squinting at her computer screen and counting.

"Shelly, did you get my file with my investigative report on the locker black holes?" he asked.

Shelly was too absorbed in her screen to answer. Theremin turned back to Newton, Mimi, and Higgy. "I cracked this thing wide open!" he said. "I investigated every single locker, and you'll never believe what I found in locker 698.17—everything that's been sucked into a

locker black hole since the lockers were installed in 1960. I even found Sven Angstrom, who went missing in 1975!"

"Wow!" exclaimed, Newton, Mimi, and Higgy.

"Hmm, that's nice," Shelly mumbled.

Theremin spun around. "Nice? Are you serious? It's the story of the century!"

Shelly looked up. "Oh, sorry, Theremin," she said. "You're right. It's a great story. I'm just struggling with this newspaper layout program. It's so slow, but it's the best one I could download."

Mimi stood up. "You're going to want to try this layout program that Crowninshield Industries developed," she said, and she walked over to Shelly and handed her a flash drive.

Shelly looked at it suspiciously.

"Oh, come on, Shelly. Give it a try," Mimi said. "It's awesome."

Shelly plugged the flash drive into her terminal and quickly downloaded the program. A template popped up on her screen.

"It's all voice activated," Mimi told her. "Just name the file you want, and tell the program where to put it. You can move photos the same way, and add headlines just by saying them."

Shelly looked doubtful, but she tried it out anyway.

"Run Theremin's black hole article on page one," she said, and the article appeared on the page. Her eyes widened and she looked at Mimi. "Wow, this is really helpful. Thank you!"

"No problem," Mimi said.

Shelly turned to Newton. "Can you go with Theremin and get some photos of that locker? And maybe of Sven, if he's around?"

"He's in Nurse Bunsen's office," Theremin reported. "He's just a little confused."

"We're on it!" Newton said, and he jumped out of his seat and grabbed the camera.

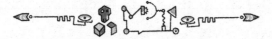

Newton took many more photos over the next two days, and was relieved not to see Flubitus in any of them. Early Wednesday morning the newspaper staff gathered around Shelly as she got ready to send out the first edition.

Shelly took a deep breath. "Here we go," she said, and she hit "publish" on the screen.

The sound of beeping tablets ricocheted around the school as the first edition of the *Franken-Sci Herald* was delivered. Shelly exhaled.

"We did it!" she said. "Let's hope everybody likes the paper."

They left the lab and made their way to the cafeteria for breakfast. When they exited the transportation tube, the first thing Newton noticed was how quiet it was. Then he realized that everyone student was absorbed in reading the newspaper, which projected in holographic form from each tablet.

"Wow!" Theremin said. "I think it's a hit, Shelly."

"We'll see," Shelly replied nervously. "Nobody's finished reading yet."

The quiet lasted for a few more minutes, and Newton and his friends (the ones with digestive systems) got their food. When they sat down to eat, they were immediately swarmed with kids, all talking at once.

"Theremin, your article was amazing!"

"Higgy, everyone knows chocolate pudding is the best!"

"Mimi, you've got to put me in your next gossip column!"

"Great photos, Newton!"

Newton smiled at the attention.

This is nice, he thought. He got excited thinking about the next edition of the newspaper and what photos he could take.

Maybe I'll become a real newspaper photographer someday, and work for one of those papers I saw when I visited Higgy in London, he thought. He'd liked that

city, with the buildings and the lights and the people. . . .

Then an anvil dropped onto his happy thoughts, smashing them.

What's the point in thinking about the future? he scolded himself. *My job in the future is to save the school. Who knows what will happen to me after that?*

Odifin wheeled over to them with Rotwang.

"Hello, everyone!" he said. "Rotwang and I were just saying that we should have volunteered to help you with the newspaper. Is it too late?"

"No," Shelly answered. "In fact, we could use some extra help to get out the Founders' Day issue."

"Excellent!" Odifin said. "We both had some ideas for you. For example, what if the information in the paper could be downloaded right into your brain, so you could absorb all of it without having to actually read it?"

"Hmm . . . ," Shelly said.

"My idea is that you could embed a video game into each issue," Rotwang said.

"Wow, could that really work?" Shelly asked.

Theremin piped up. "It's definitely possible," he said. "You know, I've been thinking too. What if we can give the newspaper the ability to have personalized front pages? We could gather data about what articles each student reads, and then program the newspaper to reorganize itself based on that student's interests."

"That's splendid!" Higgy said. "For example, my personalized paper would always have food articles on the front page."

"Exactly!" Theremin said. "I could start trying to figure out how to program it, but there's a new story I'm working on. Strange fluctuations in the school's gravitational field."

"That's weird," Newton remarked. "Sounds like it would make a great story."

"These are all amazing ideas," Shelly said. "We should definitely start working on them—but first we need to put together our Founders' Day special issue, and we only have a week!"

"Let's meet tonight and plan the issue out," Theremin suggested, and everyone started talking excitedly about what to do next.

Newton's dark mood disappeared.

Maybe the future isn't going to be great, he thought. *But right now things are pretty good!*

Founders' Day

"Wheeeeeeeeeeeeeeeeeeeeeeee!"

Newton and Higgy screamed in unison as the Dimension Destroyer sent them zipping through one dimension after another.

Whoosh! They streaked through a land of dinosaurs.

Whoosh! They zipped through deep space as a comet shot past them.

Whoosh! They hurtled through a city where cats walked on two legs, talked, and wore human clothing.

"What was that?" one of the felines asked, pointing.

Skreeeeeeeeech!

The ride came to a stop. Newton felt dizzy. Next to him Higgy's whole body was wiggling and wobbling.

"Please exit the ride," a mechanical voice instructed them.

Newton and Higgy got out of the ride car and stumbled toward the exit. Then they looked at each other and smiled.

"That was awesome!" they both said at once.

Newton took a deep breath. "Wow, when Mimi showed me the ride when it was being built, it looked impressive, but I had no idea how amazing it would be."

Higgy nodded. "Crowninshield Industries really outdid themselves," he said. "Each year they come up with something more incredible than the last. That's one reason why Founders' Day is the best day of the year!"

Newton gazed around at the festival grounds. The day was less humid than most on the island, with a gentle breeze blowing. Every student, professor, and staff member was outdoors, enjoying the festival. There were rides, like the Dimension Destroyer, the carousel, and the Customizer that Mimi had shown him. Small, colorful tents held games you could play, delicious-smelling food, and exhibits by some of the professors. And in a fenced-in area Newton saw what looked like a village, but with tiny buildings.

"What's that?" he asked Higgy.

"Mini golf!" Higgy cried. "Come on. Let's play!"

Newton followed Higgy through the crowd. They passed one of the tents, and saw Theremin there, next to a pile of monster plush toys.

"Theremin! What's all this?" Newton asked.

"Hey, guys!" Theremin said. "Well, Dad gave me a little performance boost overnight so that I would impress the founders. Turns out, the boost has made me an expert at this game."

He nodded to the wall across the counter in front of him, which was covered with balloons.

"Stand back, Melvin!" Theremin instructed the teen running the game, who quickly ducked.

Theremin's eyes glowed.

Pew! Pop!

Pew! Pop!

Pew! Pop!

Green laser beams shot out of his eyes and, with precision, popped balloons one after another. When Theremin finished, Melvin slowly stood up.

"You win," he said in flat tone. "Which monster do you want this time?"

Theremin pointed to a yellow monster plush toy hanging from the ceiling. "That one!" he cried.

"Well done!" Higgy congratulated him. "Want to come play mini golf with us?"

"No, thanks," Theremin replied. "I'm going to keep playing until I win the whole set!"

Higgy shrugged, and he and Newton went to get in line for a mini golf game. Some of the kids waiting had their tablets out and were reading the holographic special issue of the *Franken-Sci Herald*.

"That's a nice shot of the school building, Newton," Higgy remarked.

"Thanks," Newton said, smiling proudly. "I attached the camera to one of the school drones to get it."

They finally reached the entrance to the course. Higgy handed Newton a club and took one for himself.

"I'll take green, of course," Higgy said, grabbing one of the balls. "What about you?"

"Blue, please," Newton said, and Higgy handed it to him. "So how do you play?"

"Well, it's pretty much like regular mini golf, in that you travel from one hole to the next and try to get the ball into the hole with the fewest strokes possible. The person with the lowest score wins," Higgy explained. "However, what's different are the obstacles. In regular mini golf you have to hit the ball over hills, or around barriers, or through tunnels. In Mad-Scientist Mini Golf, well . . . you'll see."

Curious, Newton followed Higgy to the first hole. It was a miniature castle with an actual mini thunderstorm above it, shooting lightning and rain. A long road led across a moat to the castle.

"This one's pretty straightforward," Higgy said. "You

just have to hit the ball into the castle entrance while you watch out for the octopus."

"The octopus?" Newton asked.

Higgy placed his ball on the ground and hit it with his club. The green ball rolled down the little road.

Splash! A tentacle shot out of the water. It grabbed the ball and tossed it back at Higgy.

"Drat!" Higgy said. "See, Newton, that counts as one stroke. I have to keep trying until I get the ball into the castle."

Higgy shot the ball again. This time it whizzed past the waving tentacle and entered the castle door.

"Your turn," Higgy informed Newton.

Newton hit the ball, and it bounced into the air instead of coasting smoothly down the road. A tentacle rose from the water, caught it, and tossed it back to Newton.

"Uh, thanks," Newton said. He tried again, and this time kept the ball on the ground. The octopus grabbed the ball again, but Newton got it past the creature on the third try.

"Excellent," Higgy said, entering their scores into a small electronic scorecard. "On to the next!"

The next hole looked like a sandbox with bones sticking out of it.

"Are those dinosaur bones?" Newton asked.

Higgy nodded. "They sure are. It's a bit tricky to hit the ball through the bones, and almost impossible to get a hole in one."

"A hole in one?" Newton asked. "Are those hard to get?"

"Mostly," Higgy said. "But when you get one, it feels great."

Higgy hit the ball. It slid underneath some rib bones, then bounced off a foot bone and got stuck underneath the tailbone. He had to hit it twice more before it rolled into the hole. Newton had the same luck, and it took him four tries to get the ball in.

"Not bad, Newton," Higgy said.

The holes got a little harder as the two moved through the course, but Newton got a little better each time. He hit the ball through a moving model of planets revolving around the sun. He sank the ball into a hole on a rocket launching pad, and a real, tiny rocket shot up into the air, circled the golf course, and then landed again.

The next stop on the course was a 3-D version of enlarged particles of an atom, and the ball looped through a track and shot out into the nucleus. After that Higgy and Newton tried to hit the ball as an antigravity force held it hovering in the air.

"You're doing great, Newton," Higgy told him. "I've got twenty-one points and you've got twenty-five, but anyone could win at the last hole."

"What do you mean?" Newton asked.

They stepped in front of the last hole. Two twisting tracks that intertwined with each other snaked up the long, vertical course. There was a channel at the start of each track, but Newton couldn't see where the channels ended up. He recognized the design from his Genetic Friendgineering class—the tracks were the two strands of a DNA molecule.

"You've got to be careful where you hit the ball," Higgy said. "One strand has a channel that leads to the hole. The other strand takes the golf ball on a ride through a *worm*hole to outer space, where it's lost forever."

"Whoa," Newton said.

"If you get the ball into the hole, five points are deducted from your score, which is great because the player with the lowest score at the end wins," Higgy said. "So this is anybody's game."

Higgy placed his green ball on the course. He tapped it, and it rolled toward the DNA strand on the right.

"No, no, no. Left!" he called out, but the ball rolled into the right channel and into the twisting DNA strand.

Then it disappeared from sight, and a sound like a fog-horn blared, and the word WORMHOLE appeared on a sign above them, blinking.

"Rats!" Higgy said. "Your turn, Newton."

Newton placed the ball on the ground and aimed with his club as carefully as he could. Then he tapped the ball gently but forcefully. It zipped forward and directly into the left-hand channel.

"Whoot!" Newton cheered.

The ball rolled through the spiral, and when it dropped out of sight, a siren wailed and the words HOLE IN ONE appeared on the sign.

"You win, Newton!" Higgy cheered, holding out a hand. Newton shook the gooey appendage. "Great job!"

They deposited their golf clubs as they exited the course, and found Shelly there.

"I found you!" Shelly cried. "Newton, I need you to come with me to the main stage to take pictures of the founders' ceremony. It starts in just a few minutes."

"Sure thing," Newton said. "Want to come, Higgy?"

"I think I want to try the Customizer," he said. "I've always wanted to know what I would look like with blue goo instead of green."

"Okay. See you later!" Newton said, and then he and Shelly headed for the main stage. They passed a yellow tent with a crowd gathered in front.

"What's going on in there?" Newton wondered.

Shelly stood on her tiptoes to look over the crowd. "That's Professor Leviathan," she said.

They weaved through the crowd to get a closer look. The professor held a leash attached to a white, furry monster. The creature had a horn growing out of its nose, and wings that sprung from its back.

"Uni-teddy is the result of many years of genetic monster exploration in my lab," she was explaining. "Everybody loves unicorns. And everybody loves teddy bears. What's better than a monster that is as furry and cuddly as a teddy bear and has a unicorn horn and can fly?"

The crowd *oohed* and *aahed* as Uni-teddy, still on the leash, flew in a circle above Professor Leviathan.

"That's so cute!" Newton said, but Shelly was frowning. "What's wrong?"

"I used to like the idea of monster-making, because I love monsters and all kinds of animals," Shelly said. "But what's the point of making *new* monsters when the world is already full of monsters and animals that need help? Yes, Uni-teddy is cute, but there are plenty of kittens in the world that are just as cute, and need good homes."

"I guess I didn't think of it that way," Newton admitted. "I mean, isn't inventing new things what being a mad scientist is all about?"

"Monsters aren't *things*. They're living creatures," Shelly said.

"That's a good point," Newton agreed. This was a little surprising to hear from Shelly, who had brought him to a meeting of the Monster Club, where they made monsters. But what she was saying made sense. Shelly had a big heart and really cared about all kinds of creatures.

Shelly grabbed his arm. "Come on. We've got to get to the stage!"

An even bigger crowd had gathered in front of the main stage, and Newton and Shelly pushed their way to the very front. Three microphones had been placed in the center of the stage, and Ms. Mumtaz stood on the side, waiting to go on. Next to her, two students stood behind two brains in jars on wheeled stands, like the stand Odifin used. Their jars were encased in old-looking metal holders with engraved designs, and nuts and bolts sticking out of them.

"Are those the founders?" Newton asked.

Shelly nodded. "Yes," she replied. "Barnaby Pendergilly

and Phillipa Malagast. They sailed from England to find an island where mad scientists could perform their experiments without being persecuted."

"And those kids with them—they're seniors, right?"

"Right," Shelly replied. "Each year the top two seniors in the school get picked to wheel the founders out onstage. It's a real honor. The students also help Professor Phlegm bring the founders out of storage and zap them with electricity to wake them up."

Newton stared at the brains, floating in jars full of clear goo. "It's hard to believe they've been alive all this time."

"It's pretty impressive," Shelly agreed.

Ms. Mumtaz walked out onstage and stood before the center microphone.

"Good afternoon, students, faculty, and staff of Franken-Sci High!" she announced, and everyone stopped randomly chatting and broke into cheers. Ms. Mumtaz motioned for them to quiet down. "Before we bring out our esteemed founders, please join me in singing the school song."

Music blared through the speakers. Newton had never heard the school song before, so he listened as everyone burst out singing around him.

Light every Bunsen burner,
let every thought fly high,
for no idea is too mad here.
We are Franken-Sci High!

Experiment with courage.
No need to justify.
We revere what others fear.
We are Franken-Sci High!

Three cheers for our school!
Hurrah, hurroo, hurrai!
Our thoughts are new and we're smarter than you.
We're the excellent Franken-Sci High!

When the song finished, everyone erupted into loud cheers. Ms. Mumtaz cleared her throat.

"And now I'd like to introduce our esteemed founders, Barnaby Pendergilly and Phillipa Malagast," she said. "Today they are being escorted by two seniors, Ursula Kimoko and Solomon Pierce."

Shelly nudged Newton. "Start taking photos."

"Right," Newton said. He'd gotten so caught up in the ceremony that he'd forgotten that he was on the job.

He held up the camera, and it began to whir and spin.

Ursula and Solomon pushed the two brains up to the microphones, one on either side of Ms. Mumtaz.

"Let us begin with our annual founders' address," Ms. Mumtaz said. "First I'd like to—"

Poof!

Peewee appeared on top of Ms. Mumtaz's microphone. And he wasn't alone. He'd brought some of the other animals in the lab with him! Wingold the parrot now flew in circles around Ms. Mumtaz's head. A frog with springs for back legs hopped onto the top of Solomon's head, and the boy screamed. A rescued turtle with a titanium shell crawled along the floor.

"Oh no!" Shelly cried.

With her arms waving wildly at Wingold, Ms. Mumtaz stumbled and smacked into Barnaby Pendergilly's jar on wheels. Ursula reached out to steady the jar's stand, but tripped over the turtle and slammed into the jar instead. Barnaby zipped across the stage and crashed into Phillipa's jar. Solomon was too busy trying to get the frog off his head to save Phillipa.

Both brain stands wobbled, and then crashed to the floor. Newton watched, his mouth open in shock, as the two jars shattered into pieces, leaking goo all over the stage!

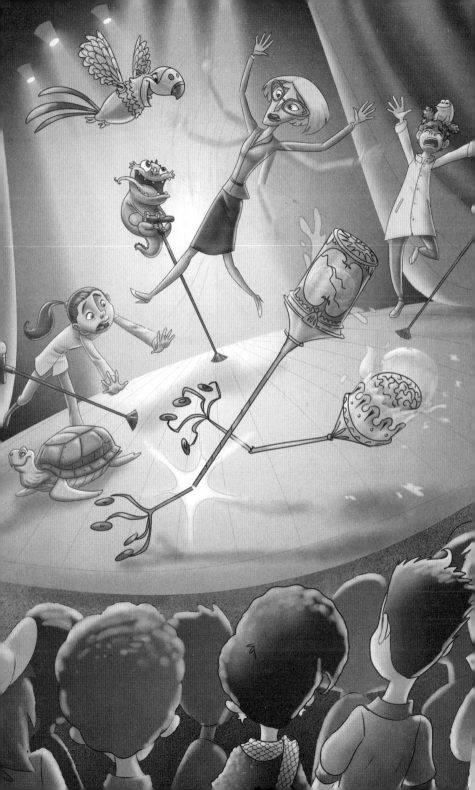

CHAPTER 7

A Monstrous Consequence

Shelly ran onstage and grabbed Peewee. Newton followed her and watched the brains starting to flop around in the goo on the floor. Then he spotted Stubbins Crouch, the custodian. Crouch was offstage, with his mop and bucket, and Newton had an idea and sprang into action.

He raced across the stage and grabbed the bucket from Crouch. Then Newton quickly dumped the soapy water out of the bucket. He scooped up the brains, one by one, with as much goo as he could, and dumped them into the bucket. He knew that brains in jars couldn't survive very long without being surrounded by goo.

Professor Phlegm ran onstage, with a drone flying next to him.

"Good work, Newton," he said. Then he clapped his hands. "Drone, get this bucket to the Brain Bank, immediately!"

The drone picked up the bucket with mechanical claws and flew off, with Phlegm running after it. Newton picked up the turtle while Shelly got the frog off Solomon's head. Wingold flew to Shelly and landed on her shoulder.

Ms. Mumtaz marched up to them.

"Shelly," she said, and her voice was like ice. "Meet me in my office in an hour."

"Yes, Ms. Mumtaz," Shelly replied quietly.

Mumtaz stormed away, and Newton gave his friend a sympathetic look.

"I'll help you get these guys back to the basement," he said.

Shelly nodded. "Thanks, Newton."

Shelly was unusually silent as they walked through the fairgrounds back into the school. In the rescue lab, Shelly set Peewee down on a table and sighed.

"I know you miss me, Peewee, but you can't just teleport to see me whenever you feel like it," she scolded in a kind voice. "And why did you bring your friends with you? I'm going to be in so much trouble."

"It wasn't that bad," Newton said. "The founders are going to be fine."

"But the ceremony was ruined," Shelly said. "And Mumtaz is not going to like that one bit."

Newton couldn't argue with that. He stayed with her and helped her give the animals water and food until it was time to go see Ms. Mumtaz.

"Well, it was nice knowing you, Newton," Shelly joked when they got to the office door. "Tell Theremin and Higgy I'll be thinking of them when Mumtaz tosses me into a black hole."

"Nothing bad is going to happen to you, Shelly," Newton replied, but he wasn't entirely sure.

Shelly turned away from him to open the door, and Newton thought fast. He closed his eyes.

Camouflage! he told himself.

When he opened his eyes, he was the same pattern as the lockers behind him. He quickly and quietly followed Shelly inside.

"Take a seat, Shelly," Ms. Mumtaz said, and his friend obeyed.

She hasn't seen me, Newton realized. *The camouflage is working!*

"Shelly, I will get right to the point," the headmistress began. "What happened today was unacceptable. After Phlegm revived the founders, they demanded a full account of the incident, and we explained to them about you and your rescue lab for animals and monsters. They demanded that we expel you from the school."

Shelly's eyes got wide. "I'm expelled?"

"I talked them out of it," Ms. Mumtaz said. "But we all agreed that we must shut down your animal rescue operation."

"No!" Shelly cried. "Why would you do that? The animals didn't do anything wrong. And Peewee wouldn't have gotten out if his box was working properly."

"Yes, I talked to Professor Leviathan about that," Ms. Mumtaz said. "She said you had plenty of time to fix the box before Founders' Day, Shelly. I told you that you could keep Peewee here if you promised to keep him out of trouble, and you broke that promise. Peewee must be returned to his natural habitat, and the animals must be set free on the other side of the island. It's best this way, to keep the school safe."

"Are you KIDDING me?" Shelly yelled. "We have lockers with black holes, and Professor Leviathan making monsters in the basement, and all kinds of things. And you're worried about some helpless wildlife?"

"I'm afraid this is how it has to be, Shelly," Ms. Mumtaz said. "And I suggest that you leave my office now, before you raise your voice again at me."

Newton, still camouflaged, moved out of the way as Shelly angrily marched past him, with tears filling her eyes. He followed her out and undid his camouflage as she disappeared around the corner.

Poor Shelly, he thought. *Ms. Mumtaz was probably just angry about what happened at the ceremony. Maybe she'll change her mind. . . .*

Newton wanted to run after her, but he didn't want to confess that he'd been spying. He typed a message to her on his tablet.

How did it go with Mumtaz?

But she didn't respond. He didn't see her again until dinnertime, when she approached him, Theremin, and Higgy at their table. Her eyes were red from crying.

"What's the matter, Shelly?" Higgy asked. "You look sad."

"I . . . I need to tell you guys something," she said. "Because of what happened earlier today, Mumtaz is making me shut down my animal rescue lab. I've got to release the animals onto the island and send Peewee back to my parents."

Theremin's eyes flashed red. "That's not fair!" he said, standing up. "I'm going to go give Mumtaz a piece of my processor right now!"

Shelly put a hand on his arm. "Don't do it, Theremin," she said. "I mean, it's nice, but Mumtaz is in a terrible mood. There's no point trying to reason with her."

She took a deep breath and looked at her three

friends. "I'd just . . . It would be nice if you could come with me before breakfast tomorrow, so I'm not alone when . . ." Tears began to stream from her eyes, and she wiped them away.

"Of course we'll be there!" Theremin said. "We're with you, Shelly."

Shelly managed a small smile. "Thanks," she said. "I'm lucky that you guys have my back."

"We'll always have your back, Shelly," Theremin promised.

"Yeah!" Newton and Higgy chimed in.

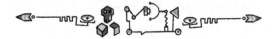

They all met in Shelly's basement animal rescue lab early the next morning. Shelly began putting all her animals into cages.

"It's too soon for them to be released," she said sadly. "I need more time to help them adapt to the improvements that I've given them. I just hope they're going to be all right."

The boys picked up the cages when Shelly had finished. She picked up the last one herself. Peewee's cage was working properly again, fixed by Professor Yuptuka late the night before. The blue monster scurried back and forth, agitated.

"I'm sorry, Peewee," Shelly said. "But this is how it has to be."

They left the lab and went outside into the bright morning sunshine. Bugs zipped by and colorful birds flew overhead as the students crossed to the other side of the island.

Shelly turned to her friends. "This is it," she said. "All you animals, listen to me. You came to me hurt, but you're all fixed now. This is your home, and where you need to be."

She opened Wingold's cage first, and the parrot flew to a tree branch and perched there.

"Sunny! Sunny!" he squawked.

Shelly smiled. "That's right, Wingold. This is real sunlight, not the artificial stuff you've been living with."

She opened the next cage. The frog with springs for legs hopped away. The turtle slowly crawled off, safe in her titanium shell. Soon, Peewee was the only one left.

Shelly sighed and looked down at Peewee's cage. "Now it's just you, Peewee," she said.

She took a school brochure out of her pocket and folded it to create a portal. A hole appeared in the air.

"Mom and Dad are expecting you, Peewee," Shelly

said. "Be good for them. And don't try to find me here! I'll come home soon and visit you."

The monster whimpered, and Shelly's eyes filled with tears. Newton took Peewee's cage from her.

"Do you want me to do it?" Newton asked.

Shelly nodded, and Newton took Peewee's cage from her and held it in front of the swirling portal.

"Good-bye, Peewee!" he said, and then he let go of the cage.

Whoosh! The portal sucked it up, and then closed.

Nobody said anything for a minute. Then Shelly spoke up.

"Thanks, everyone." Her voice sounded sad. But then, to Newton's surprise, a determined look came over her face.

"Don't forget we have a newspaper meeting today after classes," she said.

"We could certainly take a day off, Shelly," Higgy said.

Shelly shook her head. "No way. I've got something important to write about now," she replied. "In fact, I'm going to skip breakfast and start on it right away. I'll see you later!"

Shelly ran ahead of them.

Higgy's stomach rumbled. "Breakfast! I almost forgot

to eat it. I'll meet you there, guys!" And he hurried away faster than Newton had ever seen him move.

Newton and Theremin walked behind him at a normal pace.

"Poor Shelly," Theremin said. "This really stinks."

"It does," Newton said. "Maybe when Ms. Mumtaz calms down, she'll let Shelly reopen the animal rescue lab. I mean, Shelly really helped those animals!"

Then the school building came into view, and Theremin started beeping.

"Are you okay?" Newton asked.

"I'm fine," Theremin said. "Remember when I told you about the fluctuating gravity waves I was detecting? I set my sensors to go off if they detected any change in the school's gravity. That's what's happening now."

"Why would gravity be fluctuating?" Newton asked.

"I don't know," Theremin admitted. "I've also been recording some strange noises throughout the school. Something weird is definitely going on." He paused. "Do you have your camera? I'm getting a really strong signal right now. We could follow it and see if we can find out what's happening."

Newton nodded. "Yeah, I've been carrying it everywhere with me lately," he said.

Theremin opened up a compartment on his chest and

pressed some buttons. The beeping became a steady tone.

"All right. I'm locked in on the signal," he said. "Let's go."

Newton followed Theremin into the school, down one hallway, then another, and then another. Finally Theremin stopped in front of Professor Flubitus's classroom.

"Flubitus!" Newton cried. "Figures he's got something to do with this."

Newton peeked inside the classroom. He didn't see Flubitus, but there was a green, glowing light coming out of the supply closet. Theremin saw it too.

"Let's check it out," Theremin said in a low voice.

The boys quietly entered the classroom. They stood on either side of the supply closet door and tried to take a peek at what was happening inside without being seen.

The closet was no closet—it was a secret room! Inside the room was a giant, green, glowing hoop crackling with energy.

"What is that?" Theremin wondered.

Newton activated the camera, whispering, "Click!"

The camera hovered and whirred as it took pictures of the strange, green hoop. And while the

camera was photographing, something even stranger happened.

Professor Flubitus stepped out of the hoop, his hair standing on end, and his whole body sparking with electricity!

CHAPTER 8

The Flubitus Factor

Frightened that Flubitus might see them, Newton grabbed the camera and ran out of the classroom, followed by Theremin.

"What the heck was that?" Theremin wondered.

"I'm not sure," Newton admitted as they walked to their lockers. "We know Flubitus is from the future. Do you think that's a time machine?"

"It could be," Theremin agreed. "But if that's the case, then this story is dead. We're not supposed to let anyone in the school know that Flubitus is a time traveler, right?"

Newton stopped. He suddenly had an idea. "Maybe not," he said. "But you know, if the story came out, then Flubitus would have to start explaining himself. And explaining about the future . . ."

"I thought you were done trying to find out what Flubitus is up to?" Theremin asked.

"I was—I am," Newton answered. "But you're a reporter, and you caught Flubitus in the act, fair and square, right?"

It was the perfect solution. *If the whole school finds out, there'd be no point in wiping out my memory,* he thought.

"Let's ask Shelly at the newspaper meeting later what she thinks we should do," Theremin suggested.

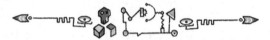

When they got to the newspaper lab that afternoon, Shelly was feverishly typing on a laptop.

"Shelly, we—" Theremin began.

"Just a few minutes, Theremin," Shelly said. "I'm almost finished with my masterpiece."

Newton and Theremin exchanged looks. Mimi, Higgy, Odifin, and Rotwang entered the lab.

"What's up with Shelly?" Mimi asked.

"Shhh," Theremin said. "She's about to reveal her masterpiece."

Shelly stood up. "I'm done!" she said. "Let me know what you think."

Then she began to read aloud:

Who Are the Real Monsters?

An Opinion Piece by Shelly Ravenholt

Some of you know that until recently I ran an animal rescue lab in the school basement, using science to help injured animals and monsters to heal and become even stronger and better.

Headmistress Mumtaz has decided that it's not "safe" to help these helpless wild creatures in our school. Yet, at the same time, Professor Leviathan is creating new monsters right here in the school!

This doesn't make any sense! There are real monsters in the world who need our help. Why can't we help them here at the school, instead of bringing new monsters into the world?

I think the reason is that the real monsters in the school are Ms. Mumtaz and any professor who doesn't think that the most important thing mad science can do is help the helpless. The real monsters are those who turn their backs on the weak and defenseless, and who only want to use mad science for profit!

I will not go to a school run by monsters. That is why I, Shelly Ravenholt, am leaving Franken-Sci High.

Shelly stopped reading.

"Shelly, no!" Theremin cried. "Are you serious?"

"You can't leave!" Newton said.

91

Shelly nodded. "I can't stay here, Theremin," she said. "I'm going to go home to my parents and Peewee, and continue my work with creatures there. Mom and Dad said they'd homeschool me."

"Shelly, I think Mumtaz is going to come around and let you help animals again," Newton said. "If you publish this, you'll only make her more upset. Why don't you stay, and wait and see what she does?"

"It's too late, Newton," Shelly said. "I'm going home tomorrow."

Mimi raised an eyebrow. "I have to say, Shelly, what you're doing is pretty brave," she said. "But I don't agree with you. There are lots of applications for mad science. It doesn't always have to be helpful. Mad science can make life easier, or more fun, and so what if it makes a profit? It *should* make a profit. Diamond-cut lasers and antigravity chambers don't grow on trees."

"That's not the point," Shelly said, agitated. "Shutting down my rescue lab was wrong. Plain wrong. And people need to know that!"

"I like what you wrote, Shelly," Odifin chimed in. "But I wish you wouldn't leave the school, just when we've become friends."

"Yeah, don't go, Shelly," Rotwang echoed.

Higgy approached her. "I'd give you a please-don't-go

hug, but I know you're not a big fan of goo on your clothes."

"Listen, you guys are all my friends—well, maybe not you, Mimi. . . . Sorry," Shelly replied. "But I've made up my mind. And you can't change it. The *Franken-Sci Herald* is yours. Print my opinion piece, or don't. I don't care!"

She stormed out, and Newton started to go after her, but Theremin put a metal hand on his shoulder.

"Let her go, Newton," Theremin said. "I've known Shelly longer than any of you have, and when she makes up her mind, it's hard to get her to change it. Especially when she's angry! Give her a chance to cool down."

Newton frowned. "There must be something we can do."

"I have an idea," Higgy said. "What if we hurry and put out a special edition of the paper with Shelly's opinion piece in it? Maybe instead of making Ms. Mumtaz angry, it will get students to take sides with Shelly. If enough people speak up, Mumtaz might change her mind about the animal rescue."

"That's an excellent idea," Odifin agreed. "I can have my report on the latest chrono-chess-ball match ready early."

"I've always got gossip to share," Mimi said.

"What about you, Theremin?" Higgy asked. "Have you uncovered any interesting surprise stories around campus?"

Theremin looked at Newton. They both knew that Mimi didn't know about Flubitus being from the future.

"We have a lead," Newton said. "We'll get on it."

"Excellent!" Higgy said. "I think I can get the hang of the layout program pretty quickly. I'll get started on putting together the issue."

Newton and Theremin left the lab.

"What now?" Theremin asked.

"Now we confront Flubitus with the photo," Newton said. "Maybe it's not a time machine, after all. Maybe it's something cool we could use for a story."

A few minutes later they found Flubitus at his desk, with his head down and fast asleep.

Theremin leaned into his face. "PROFESSOR FLUBITUS!"

The professor sat up, startled. "CHOCOLATE PUDDING VOLCANO!"

"Chocolate pudding volcano?" Theremin asked.

"Sorry. I was dreaming," Flubitus replied. "How can I help you boys?"

Newton took out the camera and showed the professor the image they'd taken of him stepping out of the hoop. The professor anxiously began to twirl the ends of his mustache.

"Theremin traced some gravitational waves or something to your classroom, and we found you coming out of this hoop this morning," Newton said. "We want to run this picture in the newspaper, but we thought we'd give you a chance to explain."

"Is it a time machine?" Theremin asked.

Professor Flubitus chuckled. "Dear boys, do you really think I would keep something as important as a time machine in my supply closet?" he replied. "This is simply a demonstration I'm putting together for my Dimensional and Interdimensional Teleportation class."

Newton and Theremin looked at each other.

"Really?" Newton asked.

"Of course," Flubitus said, rising from his chair. "Now, I am hoping to surprise the class with this, so if you wouldn't mind keeping this out of the paper, I'd appreciate it."

He didn't wait for an answer, but gently pushed them out the door.

"Okay then, shuffle along," he said, and the door slammed shut behind them.

"That was interesting," Newton said.

"Definitely," Theremin said. "I did a quick scan, and his body temperature and pulse rate indicate that he was lying."

"Typical Flubitus," Newton said. "I guess we should hold off on the photo."

"Sure," Theremin said. "Hey, I'm going to go check on Shelly. She might have cooled down by now. Would you mind letting Higgy know that we won't have a story for the issue?"

"No problem," Newton said, and the two boys walked in different directions.

Then . . . *ping!* Newton got a message notification on his tablet. He checked it. It was from Flubitus.

Meet me in Mumtaz's office NOW!

Newton sighed and walked to the office, where Mumtaz and Flubitus were waiting for him.

"I feel like we've done this already," Newton said. "You're going to tell me not to publish the picture, but the real reason is that it will change the future if I do, and you can't tell me why."

"No, Newton," Ms. Mumtaz said. "This time it's different. Professor Flubitus thinks it's time for you to know the whole truth."

"Really?" Newton asked.

"Really," Professor Flubitus said. "Newton, there is an emergency, and I see only one solution. You must travel to the future with me!"

CHAPTER 9

The Lonely Resident of Frankenstein Castle

Newton didn't say anything for a second. His brain was spinning.

"Wait, you want me to go to the future now?" he asked. "I thought . . . I thought I was supposed to wait around until the future happened and then save the school."

"Sit down, Newton," Ms. Mumtaz instructed. "Let's hear what Flubitus has to say."

Newton sat down in a chair in front of Mumtaz's desk. She sat calmly, staring at him, while Flubitus paced the floor.

"Okay," Newton said. "What's going on?"

"Once again we have reached the point in the future where the school is in danger," Flubitus began.

"How?" Newton asked. "How is it in danger?"

Flubitus looked at Mumtaz, who nodded. "It's Shelly," he revealed. "In the future she is about to reveal the secret of Franken-Sci High to the world. When she does that, future Mumtaz will have to evacuate the school and send the buildings into another dimension. It will be the end of Franken-Sci High as we know it."

Newton gasped. "So Shelly is the one who destroys Franken-Sci High?" It was hard to believe—sweet, caring Shelly, a villain! "This is awful."

Professor Flubitus nodded. "Awful indeed—"

Mumtaz interrupted. "There's something I don't understand, Hercule," she said. "This has happened in the forty-one other time lines. What is different with this time line?"

"This time I have a different solution to the problem," Flubitus explained. "I think current Newton and future Newton have a chance at stopping her—but they'll need to work together."

Newton held up his hands. "I don't even understand this whole time line thing. Can you please slow down and start from the beginning?"

Mumtaz waved her hand, and a holographic computer screen appeared in front of her face. When she tapped on an icon, a holographic scene projected into in the room. She stood up.

"Come," she said. "We'll show you."

She stepped into the projection, and Newton and Flubitus followed her. As soon as Newton stepped in, the holographic scene looked real all around him—like they had instantly traveled to a new place. They were in front of a tall, old stone castle with a moat around it. Dark clouds hovered above it, shooting jagged lightning spikes at the towers.

"Where are we?" Newton asked.

"This is the original Frankenstein castle," Mumtaz replied. "Shelly lives here now."

Newton gazed up at the creepy towers. "Shelly lives *here*?"

Mumtaz nodded. "She ends up here in every time line in the future, although sometimes it takes her longer to get here," she explained.

She snapped her fingers, and the scene changed to a room inside the castle. A woman with curly hair and big glasses sat behind a desk piled with papers. A blue monster napped on top of one of the paper piles.

It's grown-up Shelly! Newton realized. *And there's Peewee!*

"In every time line, Shelly leaves the school to protest the school's monster-making program," Mumtaz continued. "She retreats to the castle and begins taking in monsters from all over the world who need help. She refuses to talk to anyone."

Newton gazed at grown-up Shelly. Behind her glasses he saw two sad eyes.

"And then, when she learns that Crowninshield Industries is funding the school's monster-making program so that they can use monster abilities for profit, she decides to shut the whole thing down and reveal the school's secret to the world," Mumtaz explained.

"But this time line is a bit different," Flubitus chimed in. "In this time line Shelly decides to start the school newspaper so that she has an excuse to interview teachers and try to figure out your past, Newton."

"*That's* why she started the newspaper?" Newton asked.

Flubitus nodded. "Apparently. And that is why she was close to the main stage on Founders' Day, and why Peewee teleported to the stage, and why her rescue program was closed," he said. "This caused her to leave the school in freshman year. It made the Shelly in this time line sadder, and angrier. And she's also had two more years to search for monsters in the wild."

Newton digested all this. "I still don't understand what you mean about time lines," he said. "And why you needed to create me."

Mumtaz snapped her fingers again, and the scene changed. Now they were in a circular, white room, with a huge pod in the center. Men and women in white lab coats stood on a platform that went all around the room, and Newton recognized a lot of the school's professors: Leviathan, Phlegm, Wagg, a grown-up Juvinall, Wells, Rozika, Snollygoster, Yuptuka, and Flubitus. Future Ms. Mumtaz stood next to the pod, oddly looking much the same as the current Ms. Mumtaz standing next to Newton.

"After the school was evacuated and the buildings were sent to another dimension, all the professors went into hiding," the headmistress explained. "Professor Flubitus spent a few years perfecting his time-travel technology. We wanted to return to a time before the adult Shelly revealed our secret, to try to reason with her—or stop her in any way we could."

Newton got a little chill. What did "any way we could" mean?

"First we sent some of the professors back in time," Mumtaz continued. "But no one could get close to Shelly. She'd turned the castle into a fortress, and her creatures always protected her from anyone who tried to enter."

"But then we had an inspiration," Flubitus chimed in. "An inspiration directly from the science fiction book written by Zoumba Summit, also known as Mobius Mumtaz. We would create a superhuman, one who could get past Shelly's monsters and stop her."

Newton looked at the pod. "So you created me . . . in that?"

"Well, our first attempt at such a creation was not as ambitious," Mumtaz admitted. "We began with just a brain . . ."

Newton gasped. "Odifin!"

Mumtaz nodded and snapped her fingers, and the scene changed. Newton saw a brain in a jar that was smaller than the Odifin he knew. The jar was wrapped in a blanket on a table, with a teddy bear and other toys around it.

"We quickly realized that Odifin was more than just a brain. He was quite human," Mumtaz told Newton.

"We sent him back in time—fourteen years before this current time—so that he could grow up in the school," Flubitus explained. "We knew he wouldn't be an outcast at Franken-Sci High."

Newton nodded. Any problems Odifin had at the school were due to his sometimes prickly personality. For the most part nobody thought it was weird that he was a brain in a jar.

"After Odifin we began creating full humans," Mumtaz explained. "We tried forty more times, and—"

Newton interrupted her. "Wait!" he cried. "You mean there have been forty other Newtons, just like me?"

CHAPTER 10

Number Forty-Two

"Technically there have been forty-one, if you count Odifin," Mumtaz answered calmly. "But forty humans that look like you. I think we can all agree that Odifin is completely his own person."

"We came up with the idea of the bar codes to keep track of you Newtons," Flubitus explained. "The last two numbers of your bar code, Newton, are forty-two."

The scene changed again, and they were back in the white lab. A boy who looked like Newton, but a few years older, was running on a treadmill while a grown-up Professor Juvinall took notes on a clipboard.

"Newton Number Two had a few simple super-human powers, and we trained him in a lab," Mumtaz said. "But when we sent him back in time to stop adult Shelly in her castle, he wasn't strong enough to stop the monsters."

Newton watched as Newton Two was grabbed

by a giant monster claw on the castle tower.

"We kept trying," Mumtaz continued. "Newton Three, Newton Four, Newton Five . . ."

The holographic scenes kept changing. A Newton in the grasp of a large tentacle. A Newton being dragged into a hole in the ground. A Newton being carried away in the claws of a flying monster.

Newton cringed. "So I just kept failing?" he asked.

Flubitus nodded. "Not *you*, exactly, but the other Newtons—you're all a little different, you see," he answered. "Each time we sent a Newton back in time to stop adult Shelly, we created a new time line of events. When it came time to create Newton Forty-Two—that's you—I came up with the idea to do things differently."

Newton Forty-Two, Newton thought. He imagined a line of Newtons, starting with Odifin, in his head. That was a lot of Newtons!

"What's different this time?" Newton asked.

"We sent Newton Forty-Two—I mean you—further back in time," Flubitus explained. "Back to Franken-Sci High. None of the other Newtons even got to meet Shelly. We thought if you and Shelly could become friends in your youth, then maybe you could get into adult Shelly's lab without having to fend off the monsters."

Now they were in the Brain Bank, on the day when

Newton first appeared at the school. Shelly was smiling at him, and Theremin was scanning the bar code on Newton's foot.

Newton thought about this. "Okay. That part worked. Shelly and I became friends. But I haven't even visited the future yet. How do you know I failed?"

"That's where my time machine comes in," Flubitus said. "That big glowing hoop that you saw. I've been visiting the future to see how things are going. In this time line Shelly has more monsters protecting her castle than before. Future Newton is captured and being held in a monster habitat. And Shelly is working on a way to broadcast the truth about Franken-Sci high to every brain phone in the world."

"Brain phone?" Newton asked.

Mumtaz answered him. "Twenty-five years from now there are no cell phones. Instead everyone has a microchip implant in their brain. You have one too, but it only works in the future."

Newton took a deep breath. "Since my future self has failed, does that mean you're going to start another time line?"

"That is what we would normally do," Mumtaz replied.

"But I have another idea," Flubitus said. "First, I

believe that if you and future Newton combine your powers, you can work together to get past the monsters and reach Shelly. And, more important, I believe that your friendship with Shelly is strong enough to convince her to do the right thing."

"Do you really think so?" Newton asked.

"I think it's worth a try," Flubitus said. "I have to admit that the reason is somewhat personal too, Newton. This is the first time that you have been more than just a number and a fighting machine to me and the other professors. We're fond of you, Newton. We want you to succeed, not just to save the school but so that you can live happily ever after, and we won't need to create Number Forty-Three."

Mumtaz spoke up. "You have to understand, Newton, that none of this has happened to me yet either," she said. "Everything I know about the future has been shown to me by Hercule Flubitus. However, I am sure that I am as fond of you as future Mumtaz is, if not more. Now that I've heard Hercule's scheme, I like it. I think you have what it takes to succeed, Newton."

Newton mulled all this over. *Flubitus thinks I can do it. Mumtaz has faith in me. And future Shelly . . . she looks like she needs a friend.*

"I'll do it!" Newton cried.

"Excellent!" Flubitus cheered. "Let's go to my lab."

Mumtaz snapped her fingers, and the holographic projection stopped. They were back in her office, although technically they hadn't left, Newton knew. Every vision of the future they'd seen had just been a projection.

Then the headmistress leaned into Newton and hugged him. Her bony arms jabbed into his ribs, but Newton didn't mind. He was too surprised to be getting a hug from her.

She pulled away from him. "Good luck, Newton," she said. "I expect to see you back here safe, and with the problems of the future solved soon enough."

"I'll do my best," Newton promised, and he followed Flubitus to his office.

The professor closed the door behind them. Then they entered the supply closet. The giant hoop wasn't glowing yet.

"Time travel can leave you feeling a bit woozy," Flubitus warned. "But it's rather easy to do. Once the hoop is activated, you just step through."

Newton nodded. "Got it."

Flubitus flipped a switch on the wall, and the hoop began to hum and glow. It became brighter and brighter, and sparks began to sizzle from it.

"Ready!" Flubitus cried. "Follow me to the future!"

Flubitus stepped through the hoop and disappeared. Newton took a deep breath and followed.

And behind him watched a startled Theremin, who'd detected the gravity fluctuation again and had come to investigate. . . .

CHAPTER 11

Pandemonium!

Newton's body tingled as he walked through the hoop. He could feel every hair on his head standing on end. The green light blinded him for a moment, but as soon as both feet were through the hoop, the light faded. He was in the secret supply closet room with Professor Flubitus, and the hoop was no longer buzzing.

Newton frowned. "It didn't work?"

"On the contrary, Newton. It worked very well!" the professor exclaimed. "This is a time portal, not a time-and-space portal, so we are in the future in the very place where we began."

"Then how will we get to Shelly's castle?" Newton asked.

Flubitus grinned. "The same way we normally would. With a portal pass! Come, let's go see future Mumtaz!" But then he stopped. "I just remembered, Newton. There are some people in this time line who might remember you from the past, and that could cause confusion. Until we leave the school, can you use one of your abilities to change your appearance?"

"Well, I could camouflage the whole time," Newton suggested. "Or I can mimic someone if I can see an image of the person."

Flubitus hurried to his bookshelf. "I have just the thing!" he said, and he pulled out an old, leather-bound book and started flipping the pages. "My old yearbook. Here I am, at age fourteen. What do you think?"

He showed Newton a photo of a teenage boy with wild hair, a very long and wide chin, and the start of a mustache. The caption underneath read, *Hercule Flubitus wins this year's Mad Science Fair with his time portal.*

"You can be a young me!" Flubitus said, sounding tickled by the idea. "Just until we get our portal pass."

"Sure," Newton said. He stared at the photo for a moment. Then he closed his eyes and concentrated. When he opened them, Flubitus was staring at him in amazement.

"Quite remarkable, Newton!"

Newton looked at his reflection in the window, and saw young Flubitus staring back at him. He grinned. "Yeah, not bad."

Suddenly he heard a bell ring inside his head, and he jumped.

"Did you hear that?" he asked. "It sounded like it was right inside my brain."

"It was," Flubitus replied. "Remember, it's twenty-five years in the future. Things have changed. Now all school announcements and class bells get projected directly into your mind."

Newton nodded. "Wow!"

"That's not all," Flubitus said. "You may notice other things that are quite different, but try not to react. You need to blend in until we get to the headmistress's office."

Newton nodded. "Got it!"

They stepped out into the hallway. It looked the same as the school Newton knew, with lime-green-and-yellow floor tiles. Students were walking through the halls to get to their next classes. To Newton, they looked a lot like the students from his time. There were robots, like Theremin. One kid was flickering in and out of dimensions, like Professor Wells always did. A girl with cat ears and a tail reminded him of his friend Tori Twitcher, who'd once thought she was a cat.

I guess some things never change, Newton thought.

Then Newton looked more closely. All the

students were hovering inches above the ground!

"Hover shoes," Flubitus explained as they walked.

Then one of the students stepped onto a circle at the end of the hallway. His body sparkled, dematerialized, and disappeared!

"Localized teleportation pad," Flubitus told Newton. "Very handy if you're running late for class."

Next they passed a classroom door. A girl walked through it from the hallway into the classroom.

"Homework not complete," an electronic voice announced. "Report immediately to detention!"

The girl sighed and walked back into the hallway.

"Doorway homework scanners," Flubitus said. "They can also detect if you're wearing clean socks or not."

As they passed the next classroom door, Newton skidded to a stop. A boy made of green goo sat at one of the lab tables inside the room.

"Higgy?" Newton asked Flubitus. "But I thought we were in the future. Why is he still a student?"

"That's not Higgy. That's his son," Flubitus replied. He pointed into the room. "*That's* Higgy."

Newton peered farther into the room. A larger, and older, Higgy than the one he knew stood in front of the class, wearing glasses and using a pointer to

indicate calculations on a holographic screen.

"Your roommate now teaches Subversive Subatomic Physics," Flubitus informed him. "Odifin is a teacher too. Would you like to see? His class is on the way to Headmistress Mumtaz's office."

"Yes!" Newton replied, although he hesitated at the doorway for a few seconds. It was strange seeing grown-up Higgy with his son, but it made Newton happy, too.

He pulled himself away and joined Flubitus as he peered into a classroom up ahead. There was Odifin at the front of the classroom, lecturing.

"Now, students, I know that most of you know me as the *fun* professor, but brain chemistry is a serious topic," he was saying.

Seated at a desk near Odifin, working on papers, was a tall man with short, dark hair. He was wearing a spiffy suit and tie.

"That is certainly true, students," the man echoed. "A serious topic, indeed!"

"Is that . . . ," Newton began.

"It's Rotwang," Flubitus answered. "The first assistant ever to become part of the faculty here at the school. Although he *is* an assistant professor. Odifin's assistant."

"Good for him!" Newton said. "And Odifin sounds happy too."

Suddenly he heard a familiar voice in his brain.

"Attention, students, faculty, and staff!" Ms. Mumtaz began. "We've got a Code Vermillion alert! Due to circumstances beyond our control, we must evacuate the school. Please gather any essential possessions and proceed calmly to the gym for portal transport. We have only ninety minutes to evacuate. I repeat, proceed calmly!"

Students and professors began to stream into the hallways, scrambling, talking, and shrieking. Flubitus grabbed Newton by the arm.

"Quick! We must find Mumtaz!"

They ran through the crowd and then burst into the headmistress's office. Future Mumtaz looked the same as the Mumtaz that Newton knew—just like she had in the holographic projection.

"Flubitus!" she cried. "The threat from Shelly—it's happened. She's giving us ninety minutes to clear out, and she demanded that all the monsters be released onto the island. Then she will give up our secret to the world."

Then Mumtaz looked at Newton. "And who's this? Did you clone yourself or something?"

Newton took a breath and released the mimicry he was using. Ms. Mumtaz raised an eyebrow.

"Past Newton?" she asked. "Oh right! Flubitus thought you could team up with the Newton in our time line, who would be future Newton to you, and stop Shelly. I suppose you need a portal pass to the castle?"

She reached into her desk, took one out, and quickly folded it. The wind whipped up as the portal popped into existence.

"Good luck, Newton," she said. "If you fail, the school will be lost. And you'll be stuck here in the future, because the time portal will be lost too. I think we forgot to tell you that twenty-five years ago."

The realization hit Newton. "Yeah, you didn't mention that," he said. If he got stuck in the future, he'd never see Shelly, Higgy, or Theremin again. At least not the way he knew them. "I won't fail."

"Don't," Mumtaz said. "Do whatever it takes to stop Shelly."

Newton paused. "I'm not going to hurt Shelly," he said. "I don't care what she's become—she's my friend. I know she's not evil."

"She may have become evil by accident, but what she's doing is wrong," Mumtaz said. "Stop her, Newton."

Professor Flubitus handed him a school brochure.

"Use this to return when your mission is over," he said. "And I've already transmitted a schematic of Shelly's castle to your tablet. Study it when you get there, and then try to figure out where Shelly is keeping future Newton. You two will have to work together. Use your noodle noggin if you have to."

"Noodle noggin" was a code phrase that triggered superintelligence in Newton for a short period of time. Immediately Newton felt like a door was opening in his brain.

He tucked the portal pass into his pocket. "Why are you giving me this? Aren't you coming with me?"

Flubitus shook his head. "I'm no match for Shelly's monsters. You must do this alone, my boy."

Newton nodded. "I understand," he said. Then he turned and faced the portal. On the other side of that darkness was a creepy castle, an accidentally evil woman, and an army of monsters.

What am I afraid of? Newton asked himself. *After all, I'm a monster too.*

He jumped into the portal.

CHAPTER 12

Infiltrating Frankenstein Castle

He stepped out of the portal onto a cobblestone walkway. The Frankenstein castle loomed in front of him, looking very much like the castle in the miniature golf game. The walkway led to a bridge across a murky moat. Storm clouds hovered directly over the gray stone towers, shooting out jagged streaks of lightning.

Newton shivered in the damp, cold air. He needed a plan. He found the castle schematics that Flubitus had downloaded onto his tablet, a complicated blueprint with secret tunnels and entrances. But thanks to the "noodle noggin" trigger that the professor had given him, the diagram made perfect sense.

Flubitus had marked an X where he believed future Newton was being held. If Newton climbed up to the third window on the main tower, he might be able to reach the room through a hidden passageway without Shelly seeing him. First, though, he had to cross the moat. The blueprint didn't show any hidden traps, so he started to walk across.

He looked left and right at the dark, still water, and then he remembered something. The castle moat in the golf course had contained those tentacles. . . .

He heard a splash to the right of him and stopped. He turned to see a green, slimy head with one enormous eye slowly rising out of the water, staring at him.

Newton's instincts kicked in, and he instantly camouflaged with the cobblestones without having to think about it. The creature blinked. Newton stood perfectly still, trying to breathe quietly.

The head began to sink beneath the water again. Newton let out a sigh, and slowly moved forward.

Splash! A large tentacle lashed out of the water and slapped the walkway right behind him. Newton, still camouflaged, broke into a run.

Splash! Splash! Another tentacle lashed out, and then another.

Splash! Another came out, and this one made contact. It knocked Newton to the ground. Startled, Newton lost his camouflage. The tentacle quickly wrapped around him.

Newton could barely breathe. He struggled to free himself, kicking his legs.

What other abilities do I have that could get me out of this? he asked himself, but he had no answer.

The monster brought Newton right in front of its eye.

"Uh, hello!" Newton called out. "I'm a friend of Shelly's. So maybe you could just, let me go?"

The monster blinked. Then the tentacle quickly moved, smacking Newton against the surface of the water and bringing him back up.

Well, that didn't work, Newton thought.

He gazed into the giant eye again, and he had an idea. He closed his eyes for a second, concentrating, and when he opened them again, he was mimicking the monster.

The monster's eye narrowed as it studied what appeared to be a baby monster in her grasp. Confused, it let go of Newton.

He plummeted into the moat with a splash. Gills instantly sprouted on either side of his neck, and he could feel the air fill his lungs. The water was dark and murky, but his eyes adjusted, and he swam to toward the castle.

Newton climbed out and shook off the water. His reptilian DNA craved sunlight at that moment, but there was none to be found. He had to keep going and find future Newton.

According to the blueprints, he needed to get to the

main tower. He pushed his way through weeds and bushes with sharp thorns to get there.

Skree!

He looked up to see a pink monster with yellow wings and sharp claws swoop down from the sky. Newton quickly camouflaged again.

The pink monster landed in front of Newton, and this time Newton held his breath. The monster moved closer and closer to Newton, sniffing him with its furry snout. Newton knew he couldn't hold his breath much longer.

Then Newton burped. To his surprise, a cloud of green mist shot out, spraying the monster in the face. Spooked, the monster flew off.

"Well, that was new," Newton said, making a face at the taste in his mouth. "Shelly always said I probably had even more abilities than we knew. I guess she was right."

Still camouflaged, he reached the main tower. He kicked off his shoes and flexed his fingers.

"Grippy time!" he said, and he began to easily scale up the brick as his sticky fingertips and toes stuck to the tower wall.

Two wooden shutters covered the third window, and he pushed them open and peeked inside. The window

led to an open hallway, just as he'd seen in the diagram. He was in the right place.

He pulled himself inside and dropped his camouflage. A threadbare red carpet felt soft under his bare feet. He cautiously walked down the hallway and then stopped where he had seen the hidden passageway on the castle plans.

There was no doorway, only a painted portrait of a pale woman with dark hair and a frown. He lifted the picture from the wall, and saw a small door behind it.

Newton rested the portrait on the floor, opened the small door, and pulled himself into what turned out to be a secret passageway. He had to crawl on his hands and knees through the twisting path in order to fit.

Crinkle-snort!

He heard a noise in front of him, and for a second he thought about turning back. *But I can't turn back!* he thought. *I have to face whatever's coming toward me!*

Crinkle-snort!

The sound grew louder as a small, blue face came into view.

"Peewee!" Newton said in a loud whisper. "Hey there, little guy. How are you? It's good to see you."

Peewee stopped and looked at Newton.

"Do you remember me?" he asked.

Peewee squeaked and started tapping his back feet with excitement.

"How about you hang out with me for a little while?" Newton asked. "No need to let Shelly know that I'm here. I want to surprise her."

Newton had no idea if the blue monster understood him or not, but Peewee hopped up onto his back and nestled there. Newton continued to crawl. The passageway came to a dead end, and Newton pushed at the wall. A small doorway swung out and open.

Newton shimmied out and dropped down. He was in a large room with a huge glass box, almost like a zoo exhibit. He stepped up to the glass and peered inside.

A three-headed, bright blue creature hopped past him on springy legs, and he jumped back. A herd of monsters that looked like yellow puffballs bounced from plant to plant. A green creature with six legs and eyeballs on stalks scuttled across the floor.

"This looks like a monster habitat, all right," Newton said out loud. "But where's Newton?"

A skinny tree with feathery leaves suddenly transformed into a thirty-nine-year-old skinny man with black hair marked with a white streak, and green eyes.

Current Newton gasped.

It's my future self! he thought. *This is incredibly weird!*

"I'm Newton," future Newton replied. "Gotta be careful around this time of day. The Vilkrax gets hungry."

He nodded toward the six-legged creatures. Then future Newton's eyes widened.

"Hey, you look like me," he said. "Did they make another clone to come help me? Are you Newton Forty-Three?"

"Um, actually, I'm *you*—Forty-Two—but younger," current Newton replied. "Flubitus brought me here from the past."

Future Newton gasped. "Wow," he said. "I've been studying up on time travel for the last twenty-five years, and I thought that, you know, both of us couldn't be in the same place and time, or the world would explode or something."

Both Newtons stared at each other for a moment, waiting.

"I guess that's not going to happen," current Newton said. "Anyway, I came to get you out of here."

Future Newton shrugged. "I don't know how. If I can't get out of this glass box, then I don't think you can get in."

"Is there an entrance?" current Newton asked. "How did Shelly put you in here?"

"There's a door," future Newton said, pointing. "Shelly comes in with food and stuff once a day. She uses a key."

Current Newton found the door and yanked on it. "Locked!" he reported.

"I could have told you that," future Newton said.

Current Newton thought. "Maybe I can just sneak into wherever Shelly is and get the key," he said.

Future Newton shook his head. "That won't be so easy. Her office is guarded by a gauntlet of monsters, each one tougher than the last. How do you think I ended up in here?"

"I know," current Newton said. "But I've got to try. If I don't, Franken-Sci High will be gone forever. And I'll be stuck here in the future."

Current Newton had almost forgotten about Peewee, who was still on Newton's back. The little monster began to chatter excitedly. Then *poof!* He vanished.

"Oh great," future Newton said. "He's probably gone to tell Shelly you're here!"

Current Newton sighed. "Sorry," he said. "I guess I—"

Poof! Peewee appeared on current Newton's back again, and then moved up to Newton's shoulder to show Newton that he was holding a key in his paws.

"Wow, thanks, Peewee!" Newton said, and he approached the door. "This is all you need to open it? Not a key card, or an eyeball, or DNA?"

Future Newton shrugged. "Everything in this castle in pretty old school. Shelly likes it that way."

Then he looked behind him. The Vilkrax was trotting toward him, licking his lips.

"Would you mind hurrying up and opening the door?" future Newton asked.

"Oh sure," current Newton replied, and he scrambled to open it up. Future Newton slipped out and slammed the door behind him. Current Newton locked it again.

"Thanks," future Newton said. "Okay. Now we should get out of here." He headed toward the passageway that current Newton had come through.

"Wait!" current Newton cried. "We've still got to find Shelly and stop her. We're running out of time."

Future Newton shook his head. "It's no use. I try talking to her every time she brings me food. She won't listen."

Current Newton frowned. "But you two are friends. Why won't she listen? Why did she lock you in here?"

Future Newton anxiously scratched his head. "Well,

it might have something to do with the fact that I went to work for Crowninshield Industries."

"You WHAT?" current Newton asked. "But you know how Shelly feels about Mimi."

"I thought I was being smart!" future Newton cried. "I knew Shelly was against Crowninshield's monster experiments. I thought if I worked for them, I could convince Mimi to maybe stop the program. Or use rescued monsters. But Mimi wanted to do it her way, and Shelly got mad."

"We still have to try," current Newton said. "Maybe she'll listen to the two of us."

Future Newton sighed. "Fine," he said. "But don't be surprised if we both end up in that cage again. At least I'll have someone to talk to."

Current Newton looked at the diagram. "Looks like there's a passageway that goes directly to Shelly's lab," he said. "Maybe we can bypass the monster gauntlet if we use it."

He walked ahead and made a right into another hallway, followed by his future self. There, on the wall, was a portrait of the same sour-faced woman.

Peewee started to chatter excitedly.

"Thanks so much for the key, Peewee," current Newton said. "I think you gave it to us because you

want us to help Shelly. That's what we're going to do."

Peewee chattered even more loudly as current Newton took the picture off the wall. He hoisted himself up, climbed in through the hole . . .

. . . and began to plummet downward at rocket speed!

The Lucky Ones

Current Newton plummeted down a chute.

Thump! He landed on a hard stone floor.

"Get out of the wayyyyyyyy!" came a voice from behind him, and Newton rolled to the right as future Newton shot out of the chute.

"Ouch!" future Newton complained. "That's hard on the old knees."

"Old knees? Aren't you only thirty-nine?" current Newton asked.

Then a shadow crossed over them. A shadow with curly hair. Both Newtons looked up to see future Shelly looming over them. She wore a white lab coat, and her eyes glared at them through her goggles.

She looks different from how she did in the projection Flubitus showed, current Newton thought. *In that she just looked like a grown-up. Now she looks . . . like a mad scientist! A really mad scientist!*

Peewee climbed off current Newton's back, and joined Shelly as she sat down on a big, plush chair.

"Well, well, well," Shelly said, looking at future Newton. "What have we here? Looks like you've escaped, Newton! And who is your little friend here?" she said, looking at current Newton. "A clone?"

Current Newton jumped to his feet. "Shelly, it's me!" he said. "I'm Newton too—the Newton you knew in school. I've come from the past to save the future."

Shelly threw back her head and laughed.

"Ha, ha, ha, ha, HA, HA, HA!" she cackled. "Was this that fool Flubitus's plan from the beginning? Is this what he meant when he said that the two of us had a big role to play in the future of Franken-Sci High? Ha, ha, HA!" She stopped laughing and looked at Newton. "Seriously, was this his plan all along? To send you here to stop me? Because it won't work."

"You're right," current Newton said. "It doesn't work. They've sent me to stop you forty times before this—forty-one if you count the Odifin experiment—and I've failed."

"I'm not surprised to hear that," she said. She began pacing back and forth. "But why keep trying? It's not like I'm hurting anyone. Ninety minutes is plenty of time to evacuate the school."

She looked over at a bank of computer screens, where a digital countdown flashed next to a big, red button and a big, green button. "More like nineteen minutes now. Everyone will be safe—including the helpless monsters being created to make money to line the pockets of Crowninshield Industries. And the school's evil experiments will be done with, forever."

Future Newton spoke up now. "Shelly, it's like I've been trying to tell you. The monsters are treated well. By destroying the school, you'll be destroying all the amazing learning that happens there. So many inventions are coming out that will really help the world."

"Blah, blah, blah," Shelly said. "I've heard it all before from Mumtaz. Soon everyone in the world will know about the existence of Franken-Sci High. Its dark secrets will finally see the light!"

Future Newton threw up his hands. "See what I mean?" he asked current Newton. "You can't reason with her."

"No, you can't, when your reason is faulty," Shelly said. She marched over to a door made of metal bars. "And since you can't reason, I'll need to keep you busy with a monster battle so you don't try to stop me." Behind the bars on the door, something growled.

Future Newton sighed. "Don't bother, Shelly. You know I would never hurt you. You're my friend."

Something flickered in Shelly's eyes. "Nice try, traitor," she said. "No friend of mine would go work for Mimi."

She moved to open the door again.

Crinkle-squark! Peewee looked at Newton and started chattering.

"Wait!" current Newton cried. "If you won't listen to reason, maybe you'll listen to something else."

Shelly eyed him. "Like what?"

Current Newton turned to future Newton.

"Do you remember that day, after Professor Flubitus accidentally turned Peewee into a giant monster, and we brought Peewee down to the lab with Theremin and Shelly?" current Newton asked.

Future Newton shook his head. "Not really."

"Come on!" current Newton urged. "Use your noodle noggin!"

Future Newton grinned. "I remember," he said, and then he transformed into young Shelly. Future Shelly froze, seeing her younger self.

Current Newton, and future Newton as young Shelly, repeated the conversation from that day.

"Poor guy," future Newton said in young Shelly's

voice. "He was lost and alone when I found him, and scared."

"Peewee was lucky that he found you," current Newton said to young Shelly. "And I guess I was too."

"I think Theremin and I are the lucky ones," said young Shelly. "This place has gotten a lot better since you showed up."

Current Newton looked at young Shelly. "Franken-Sci High isn't just about inventions and ideas," he said. "It's a safe place for kids like me. Kids like you, and Theremin, and Higgy, and Odifin, and Rotwang."

As current Newton spoke, future Newton transformed into each one of their friends from the past.

As she watched them act out the past, future Shelly sat down in her chair. Tears started to form in her eyes.

"No!" she said, wiping them away. "This is a trick!"

Current Newton knelt down in front of her. "It's not a trick, Shelly," he said. "I was just at the school a little while ago. Some things have changed, but the kids haven't. They're weird and cool and strange and wonderful. And if those kids have to go back to the real world, they won't have any friends, nobody who understands them."

"I—I know—" Shelly stammered. "But—what about the monsters? Monsters that didn't ask to be created, monsters that are going to be sold by Crowninshield Industries so that people can profit off their powers? Mumtaz won't listen to me."

Future Newton changed his appearance to stop looking like young Shelly. Once he was back to his usual thirty-nine-year-old self, he spoke up. "I think Mumtaz's hands are tied," he said. "The school can't survive without Crowninshield Industries. Mimi is the key, and that's why I've been working for her. I'm trying to change things from the inside, Shelly. You have to believe me."

Shelly didn't say anything.

"Stop the countdown, Shelly," current Newton said. "I promise we'll find a way to stop the monster program. If we don't, you can come back here and do what you need to do. I won't stop you."

Shelly looked at current Newton. "I missed all of you when I left the school, you know," she said. "And you reached out, and so did Theremin and Higgy and Odifin and even Rotwang. But I was so angry, and so hurt. I didn't want to talk to anybody. And I've been that way ever since."

"We're all still your friends, Shelly," future Newton promised.

"Yeah. We're the Goo Getters, remember?" current

Newton asked, reminding Shelly of the group name the friends had used when they'd competed in the Brilliant Brains Trivia Competition.

Shelly laughed. "Yeah, the Goo Getters."

She swirled around in her chair and pressed the red button. The countdown stopped.

Crunkle-squee!

Peewee leaped out of the chair and started running in happy circles. Shelly smiled.

"This is the first time I've seen you happy in a long time, Peewee," she said, and she stood up. "Okay. Let's see if we can stop the monster project. What's our first step?"

Future Newton took a device out of his pocket. "If you can lower your portal shield, we'll go talk to Mimi," he said.

Shelly frowned. "If she hasn't listened to you before, why do you think she'll listen to us now?"

Future Newton gazed over at current Newton and grinned.

"I think Flubitus knew what he was doing when he sent this kid here."

CHAPTER 14

Mimi's Monsters

Shelly deactivated the portal shields inside the castle, and future Newton pressed a button on his device. A portal opened up.

"This goes directly to Crowninshield Industries," he said. "Every employee gets one. Makes for an easy commute. Come on!"

Future Newton jumped through the portal. Current Newton held back.

"You're making sure I go with you, aren't you?" Shelly asked.

"Yup," current Newton said.

Shelly grinned. "I haven't seen Mimi in twenty-five years. This isn't going to be easy."

"The Shelly I know was never afraid to do something because it wasn't easy," Newton said.

Shelly nodded and stepped into the portal, and Newton followed her.

They emerged on the funicular platform. Newton looked up at the building on top of the mountain, which had expanded into the clouds. Several white, boxlike buildings floated in the sky around and above the original building.

"Mimi has always been a fan of antigravity," future Newton explained. "Come on. We can go directly to her office."

He moved away from the train platform to a circular pad. He stepped onto a cloud-shaped mat.

"Up!" he cried, and the mat lifted him upward and carried him toward the building that was higher up in the sky than all the others.

"Ugh," Shelly said. "I hate heights." She stepped onto another cloud-shaped mat and closed her eyes. "Up!"

Current Newton followed her. Once they'd reached the top, Shelly stumbled as she stepped off her mat, and future Newton grabbed her hands.

"Thanks," she said. "You know, I've never apologized for locking you in that monster habitat. I was planning on letting you out after I finished destroying the school."

Future Newton grinned. "That's some apology."

Shelly frowned. "Sorry, Newton. I'm not good at the whole being-around-humans thing."

"You were good at it when I first met you," future Newton replied. "That's why I forgive you."

Current Newton stepped off his mat onto the landing ledge. "Okay, what are we going to tell Mimi?" he asked. "Is there a plan?"

"Nope," future Newton said cheerfully. "But this is our only chance to stop Shelly from her evil plan. Right, Shelly?"

"Um, right!" Shelly replied.

Future Newton walked from the landing ledge to the door of the building. He breathed onto a red square to the left of the door. It turned green, and the door slid open.

A woman with blond hair sat behind a desk. Her eyes widened as the three of them walked inside.

"Newton, what are you doing here?" she asked.

"Well, Mimi—" future Newton began, and current Newton realized that they were in future Mimi's office.

"Not you!" Mimi snapped. "You!"

She pointed at current Newton.

"I'm him, from the past," current Newton explained.

Mimi rolled her eyes. "Duh. I figured that out," she said, standing up and walking around the desk. "But what exactly are you doing *here*?"

"I'm here to help save Franken-Sci High," he replied.

"Duh. I know that, too," she said. "But what do I have to do with it?"

Shelly spoke up. "Really? You have to ask? You're the whole reason for this problem."

"Oh, hi, Shelly," Mimi said. "How's the whole evil thing going?"

Shelly turned around as if to leave. "This is pointless!"

"Shelly's not evil," current Newton said. "She just cares about monsters. And people. She's agreed not to give up the school's secret."

"*If* Mimi stops the monster program," Shelly chimed in, turning back to face Mimi.

Mimi nodded. "See, now, that's the thing," she said. "I didn't get to be the head of Crowninshield Industries because I caved to other people's demands. There's no way I'm going to do something just because somebody threatens me."

"Well, *I* didn't threaten you, Mimi," future Newton said. "I've been asking you to rethink this monster thing for the last year. But you didn't want to listen."

"I can explain," Mimi said. "It's kind of funny, actually. I came up with the monster program as a way to save the school."

"Wait, what?" current Newton asked.

"Well, it all started that day I was eavesdropping on

you when you were in Mumtaz's office with a bunch of professors," Mimi began. "I was convinced from the day you came to the school that you were a spy sent to get to know me and infiltrate Crowninshield Industries."

Current Newton's eyes widened. "So you heard what I couldn't tell my friends—that the professors had created me in the future to save the school?"

Mimi nodded. "Then I invited you here so I could body scan you, to find out what they had done to you."

Current Newton's eyes got even wider. "I thought you were just being nice."

"Ha!" Shelly said. "I knew it!"

"Well, I was *partly* being nice," Mimi said. "And partly curious. And I found out that Newton had all these amazing abilities, and it got me worried about what the professors had said. If the school was in real danger, what was one guy with grippy fingers supposed to be able to do about it?"

"Now, that's a tiny bit insulting," future Newton chimed in.

"No offense, Newtons," Mimi said. "Anyway, I asked my parents to help fund a special monster program at Franken-Sci High to help create monsters that could *really* protect the school in case something went wrong."

Shelly shook her head. "If that's true, then why are you planning on selling monsters?"

"It was a logical extension of the program," Mimi said. "A glow-in-the-dark underwater monster with high intelligence is the perfect assistant for a deep-sea diver. A monster that generates electricity can power a lab. A flying monster can gather data from high altitudes without needing oxygen—"

"Yes, monsters are amazing," Shelly said. "But you can't just force them to do things without asking them. And you don't need to make new monsters to do those things. There are already monsters in the world that need good homes."

Current Newton and future Newton spoke at the same time.

"That's the answer!" they said.

"What do you mean?" Mimi and Shelly asked in unison.

"You can—" both Newtons said together.

"I mean, you both—" the Newtons said.

They both stopped.

"You say it," future Newton offered.

Current Newton nodded. "Mimi, if you stop making new monsters, the school will be safe," he said. "And you and Shelly can work together to help the monsters that you created, and the ones Shelly has found. Shelly knows how to communicate with them, and she can find out if they want to do jobs like the ones you talked about."

He looked at his future self. "Is that what you were going to say?"

Future Newton nodded. "Basically," he said. "I was also going to offer to work on the program with you both. As a sort of, mediator."

Mimi and Shelly looked at each other.

"That's smart thinking, Newtons," Mimi finally said. "Especially the part about you being a mediator. Back at school, liking Newton was the only thing Shelly and I had in common."

"What about you, Shelly?" current Newton asked. "Are you up for this?"

She frowned thoughtfully. "No more new monsters?" she asked.

"No more," Mimi promised.

"And you won't make monsters do jobs they don't want to?" Shelly asked.

Mimi shook her head. "Promise. But I hope you'll convince them to work—for pay, of course. If I were a monster, I'd want to use my powers to do things. I bet it will give them confidence and make them feel useful."

"It just might," Shelly agreed.

At that moment a bright light flashed in the room.

"Everybody smile and say 'circuit breaker'!" Theremin said as he burst through the door. At least, to current Newton, it looked like Theremin. But his voice was much deeper.

"Theremin!" Mimi cried. "Have you been spying on us?"

"Not spying. Reporting," he shot back. "The whole mad-scientist world is freaking out about Franken-Sci High possibly being sent to another dimension, and there's only a minute left!"

"But I stopped the countdown!" Shelly cried.

"Did you tell Mumtaz?" Theremin asked.

Shelly frowned. "Whoops!"

Mimi waved her hand in the air, and a screen appeared in front of her face.

"Get Mumtaz!" she said, and a hologram of the face of the headmistress appeared.

"Mimi, what is it?" Mumtaz asked. "I'm about to send the school into another dimension!"

"You don't have to," Mimi said. "Shelly and I worked it out."

Mumtaz raised her eyebrows. "Really?"

Shelly stood next to Mimi and waved. "Yeah, um,

sorry about all that. I'm not going to give up the school's secret."

Flubitus appeared behind Ms. Mumtaz.

"Is young Newton there? Tell him to get back here right away!" Flubitus said. "Now that the school is saved, we can't risk altering this time line any further."

"I'll send him back through the direct portal," Mimi promised, and then she pressed a button, and the hologram faded.

Theremin turned to current Newton. "Hey, good to see you, man. You know, you were a lot more fun when you were back in school." He pointed to future Newton. "This guy is a real bore."

"Hey!" future Newton protested. "Maybe it's because I've been worried about saving the school for the last twenty-five years."

"Well, um, I guess this is good-bye," current Newton said, looking at the adult versions of his friends. Even though things had worked out, he could see the sadness in Shelly's eyes, and it worried him.

"One question," he said. "If I go back to the past, I'm gonna know that all this stuff is going to happen. But what if I try to change it, before it gets . . . before Shelly gets accidentally evil? Will it cancel out this time line?"

"I'm not sure," future Newton said. "But based on

what I've researched, I don't think so. This time line has already been created, so we'll all keep moving forward in it. When you go back to the past, you might end up jump-starting a whole new time line."

"I might need my noodle noggin to figure all this out," current Newton said.

Mimi motioned to a teleport pad in her office. "Step right up, Newton. This will take you directly back to school."

Current Newton walked onto the pad. "It's weird," he said. "I'm going to miss you guys."

"That's just silly," Mimi said. "We'll all be there."

Except maybe for Shelly, current Newton thought.

"Hey, dude," Theremin said. "Now that you know that everything works out, maybe you can lighten up a little bit? Don't end up like this guy."

"Hey!" future Newton said.

Current Newton grinned. "I'll try," he said. "Ready to go, Mimi!"

"Bye, Newton!" Mimi said, and the others waved as he dematerialized in front of them.

He rematerialized back in future Ms. Mumtaz's office. Flubitus enveloped him in a hug.

"Well done, my boy. Well done!" he cried.

"It was your idea to bring me here," young Newton

said. "I'm just glad it worked out."

"I suppose I'll have to un-evacuate everyone," future Ms. Mumtaz said with a sigh. But then she smiled. "Nice work, Newton."

Newton and Flubitus walked through the empty halls of the school back to the time hoop. The professor activated it, and they both stepped through.

Newton blinked as the green flow faded. Then he heard a voice.

"Aha! I knew there was something up with this machine!"

CHAPTER 15

The Future Is So Bright,
You Gotta Wear Diode Laser Goggles

Theremin, Shelly, Higgy, and Mimi were all in the supply closet.

"It's a time machine!" Theremin continued. "I heard Flubitus say you were going into the future! So I told Shelly and Higgy, and they came and we waited for you."

"And of course I was spying, so I followed them in," Mimi said matter-of-factly.

Newton and Flubitus looked at each other.

"We can't lie," Newton said.

"But we have to be careful," Flubitus added. He turned to the four other students. "Let's all go to Ms. Mumtaz's office and discuss this calmly."

They quickly made their way to the office, where the headmistress was eagerly waiting. She raised an eyebrow at the sight of Newton's friends.

"What's all this?" she asked.

"Young Theremin is a very intrepid investigative

reporter," Flubitus answered. "I'm afraid they know of our travels."

"What happened?" Mumtaz asked. "If Newton is back, that means . . ."

"The school is safe in the future," Flubitus finished.

Mumtaz let out a breath. "Wonderful," she said. She looked at Newton and his friends. "Now, you saved the school, and we're so very grateful, but I must ask that you try to carry on as usual and focus on being students again."

Newton had been thinking about what he would say at this very moment. His noodle noggin had been helpful. But also he felt more confident. He'd faced monsters. He'd rescued his future self. He'd saved the school.

I can do this, he thought.

"A few things need to change," Newton said. "For one thing, Ms. Mumtaz, you have to let Shelly keep rescuing animals and monsters. And bring Peewee back. If it wasn't for him, we would have lost the school."

"Wow, really?" Shelly asked.

"But—" Mumtaz began.

"There are enough geniuses at this school to help figure out how to keep all the animals from escaping," Newton said. He looked into her eyes. "Trust me. It will make the future a whole lot better."

Mumtaz nodded. "Consider it done."

Newton turned to Shelly. "You have to stay," he said.

"I will, if I can run the rescue lab," she replied.

"And there's one more thing," he said. "I have an idea about how to make the world better for monsters, too. But you'll have to work with Mimi."

Shelly glanced at Mimi. "If it will make the world better for monsters, I'll do it."

Mimi frowned. "Hmm . . ."

"Come on, Mimi," Newton urged. "Do it for the future."

Mimi nodded. "I'll give it a try, Newton," she said.

Flubitus clapped his hands. "Splendid!" he cried. "I feel we are looking at a very bright future indeed. How does that song go? The future's so bright, you must wear . . ."

"Diode laser goggles?" Theremin suggested.

"That's it!" Flubitus cried.

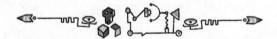

"Okay, Newton. Turn left. Now smile. Don't hunch your shoulders so much. . . . Hold it. Click!"

Newton posed in front of the wall in the newspaper lab as Theremin tried to take his photo.

"I like it a lot better when I'm working the camera,"

Newton protested.

"Just a few more," Theremin said. "After all, you're the star of my new front-page article, 'The Boy Who Saved the School.'"

Higgy came over. "Tell me again about what we're like in the future? Am I really a professor?"

Newton nodded. "Yes, but like I told you, that's a whole other time line. Things could be different in the future for all of us." He glanced over at Shelly. "But I hope, different in a good way."

Shelly and Mimi were sitting at a computer terminal together, working on Newton's idea.

"Your family really knows how to find monsters in the wild?" Mimi was asking.

Shelly nodded. "It's our main specialty. And if Crowninshield Industries builds a monster rescue center on the island, we can bring all the stray monsters we find here."

"And then we can test them, to see what powers they have," Mimi went on. "Just like you did with Newton?"

"Right!" Shelly said, smiling. "But only if the monsters agree to it."

It's good to see Shelly so happy! Newton thought. His noodle noggin couldn't tell him if the seeds he'd planted in the present would mean a better future for

Shelly, but something in his gut told him they were all on the right track.

Professor Flubitus walked into the newspaper lab. Today his wild green hair was tamed by the strange bowler hat he often wore, topped with an assortment of unusual gadgets.

"Hello, students," he greeted them. "I just came to—whoa!"

Peewee teleported into the room, and Professor Flubitus tripped, trying to avoid him. The bowler hat flew off his head and landed on a lab table. A gadget on the hat began to project a huge digital image into the air.

"It's a newspaper!" Theremin cried. *"The Mad Science Monitor."*

"And look!" Mimi cried, pointing. "The date is twenty-five years from now."

"Oh dear," Flubitus said, sitting up on the floor. "I brought this back with me from my latest travels and—"

Peewee jumped onto his shoulder. Flubitus laughed. "Oh my, that tickles!"

While Peewee kept the professor busy, the friends scanned through the issue.

"No way! I'm the editor in chief!" Theremin cried.

"Well," Mimi said, pointing to an article, "I'm head of

Crowninshield Industries in the future, just like Newton said."

There was a photo of Higgy, his wife, and his son at the Franken-Sci High Annual Parabola Picnic.

"My future family!" Higgy gasped.

Newton read the photo credit, "'Photo by Newton Warp-Ravenholt,'" he said. "But 'Ravenholt' is Shelly's . . ."

Shelly blushed. "There's a feature article on the monster rescue center here, run by Shelly Ravenholt-Warp."

"Oh," Newton said, and he blushed too.

"I don't get it," Theremin said.

"Duh, it means they get married in the future," Mimi said.

Flubitus jumped to his feet. "Enough, enough!" he said, and he grabbed the hat, turned off the projector, and put the hat back on his head. "Carry on!"

The friends all looked at one another for a minute, not sure what to say.

"I think we should stop worrying about the future from now on," Shelly said.

"Yes," Newton agreed. "Let's just have fun getting there."

Pfffffffffft! Higgy made a farting noise with his feet.

"Ew!" Mimi wailed.

"Just getting us started," Higgy said, and everyone laughed. "Living in the present, you know?"

Newton looked around at his happy friends, and for the first time, he knew in his head, and his heart, and in every cell of his weird DNA, that things were going to be all right.

Guess I'd better get some diode laser goggles! he thought.

Epilogue

During the first week of sophomore year, Newton, Shelly, and Theremin met in the library Brain Bank.

"Leave it to Wagg to give us an assignment on the first day of school," Theremin complained.

"At least he's letting us work in teams," Shelly said. "Come on. Let's plug in."

Newton plugged one end of a cord into his tablet, and the other end into a port on a tank of one of the brains—Sir Isaac Newton.

"Hello, Sir Isaac," Newton began.

The brain's eyestalks moved so that the eyeballs focused on Theremin. "You!" he cried. "You're the creature who knocked me out of my jar last year! You were almost the end of me!"

"It was an ACCIDENT!" Theremin yelled.

Newton and Shelly looked at each other and shook their heads. This wasn't going to be easy. . . .

In the aisle of brains behind them, a light flashed, but Newton, Shelly, and Theremin didn't see it. A boy appeared out of thin air.

The boy was tall and thin, with green eyes. His black hair had a white streak down the middle. He wore a blue shirt, jeans, and sneakers. And he was barefoot. On the bottom of his left foot was a bar code that ended in the number seventeen.

The boy peeked through the brains on the shelf and spied Newton, Shelly, and Theremin on the other side. A slow grin spread across his face. A grin that most people would have called an evil grin if they'd seen it.

It worked! Newton Seventeen thought. . . .